Callie P

"Fran Rizer's Callie Parrish and St. Mary, S.C., are as southern as fried chicken and sweet tea— and just as delightful."
____Walter Edgar, *Walter Edgar's Journal,* SCETV Radio

"A lively sleuth who manages to make funeral homes funny."
____Maggie Sefton, Author of the Molly Malone Suspense Mysteries and the Kelly Flinn Knitting Mystery Series

"Callie Parrish is a hoot! I laughed so hard I dropped my book in the bathtub."
____Faith Hunter, Author of the Jane Yellowrock series

"Fran Rizer is on target—and spectacularly so— with her latest Callie Parrish mystery, a story a bit less cozyesque than previous Callie Parrish books but so compelling that even longtime fans will be captivated by the twists and turns."
____Jerome Spencer, *Cozy Reviews*

"Fun and flamboyant!"
____Dorothy Hawkins, *Mystery, Mystery*

PREVIOUS BOOKS BY FRAN RIZER

The Callie Parrish Mystery Series

A Tisket, a Tasket,
A FANCY STOLEN CASKET

Mortuary cosmetician Callie Parrish likes to end her days in a relaxing way—with a Moon Pie and a mystery book, but then car dealer Bobby Saxon comes into the funeral home with a hypodermic needle hidden in his neck. Callie realizes there's a killer on the loose trying to bury some deadly crimes. Callie's got a knack for making the dead look their best, but no amount of concealer can cover up murder.

Hey, Diddle, Diddle,
THE CORPSE & THE FIDDLE

Little Fiddlin' Fred might be tiny in stature, but he's huge in the bluegrass world. When his dead body tumbles out of a bass case on-stage, the festival erupts in chaos. Local cops advise Callie not to get involved, but when Jane discovers a second corpse and then vanishes, Callie has no choice but to investigate the murders and her best friend's disappearance.

Rub a Dub, Dub, DEAD MAN IN A TUB
Published as CASKET CASE

St. Mary's beloved pharmacist is found float-
ing facedown in his hot tub. Callie Parrish
wonders if the kind man died of natural
causes, or if his seemingly distraught young
wife had a hand in his demise, but the pharmacist's death is only the first untimely death
to keep Middleton's Mortuary busy. Is the
apparently psychotic man who has become
obsessed with Callie a killer or is Callie in the
middle of two extremely puzzling cases?

Twinkle, Twinkle, Little Star
THERE'S A BODY IN THE CAR

When Callie finds a car with an unidentified
dead man and a poisonous snake locked
inside, she's busy caring for her sick father
and helping with her brother Bill's wedding—
too busy for any detecting. The next client who
winds up on Callie's work table died the very
same way. Two elderly men—both dead from
poisoning. Callie vows not to get involved, but
when her brother Frankie is poisoned, also,
and the sheriff goes missing, Callie jumps right
in.

Mother Hubbard Has
A CORPSE IN THE CUPBOARD

Callie confronts the slayer of an unidentified youth inexplicably killed in a cupboard at the county fair when she, Jane, and Rizzie are enjoying a girls' day out. When Maum's surgeon is fatally shot, Rizzie's younger brother Tyrone is accused of homicide, throwing Callie into the middle of an investigation that leads to a new romance while taking her into the world of gangs. Her involvement could land Callie in a casket with her name spray-painted on it.

A CORPSE UNDER THE CHRISTMAS TREE

Callie and her BFF, Jane, love presents anytime, but what they find beneath their gorgeous Christmas tree isn't a gift from Santa Claus. It's Santa in person—murdered and dumped beneath the tree Callie and Jane decorated with much joy for the holiday season. The sheriff makes Callie a temporary undercover deputy. She finds clues at Safe Sister and at a turkey trot, but can she solve the case before the killer identifies both Callie and Jane as the next victims?

Hickory, Dickory, Dock,
MURDER IS ON THE CLOCK

Callie doesn't have time to sleuth the day before her father's wedding though Jane's accusation that Callie attracts murder like a magnet seems true. She finds a John Doe homicide victim.

Jane and Callie are terrified when they begin receiving threats from a man who knows Jane is telephone fantasy actress Roxanne and where she lives. Their fear is amplified when he begins making veiled threats toward both of them.

John Doe is identified—Loose Lucy's ex-boyfriend. Callie is astonished to learn her brother Bill has hidden Lucy in the same house he lives in with his wife. The sheriff vows Bill is not a suspect, but he wants to talk to him. Instead of cooperating, Bill runs.

Callie is torn between protecting Jane from her stalker and investigating the murder. She believes Jane is in real danger, but she knows the only way to save Bill is to find the killer herself—though Callie doubts anyone can save her brother's marriage.

ALSO BY FRAN RIZER

SOUTHERN SWAMPS & RUINS

These twenty-one haunting tales, all set in South Carolina, are guaranteed to leave readers sleepless. Fifteen of the stories are by Fran Rizer and her collaborator, author of *Wounded,* Richard D. Laudenslager. The other six are by guest authors Michelle Thomas Cox, Jenifer Boone Lybrand, Nathan R. Rizer, J. Michael Shell, Robert D. Simkins, and Two Ravens.

KUDZU RIVER
A Thriller of Abuse, Murder, and Retribution

Someone is carving a bloody trail of dead teachers along the S. C. coast. He targets Teacher of the Year Katie Wray and her friend Samantha Branham. A lifelong victim, Tennessee Linda sees the killer, but haunted by her past, her dead parents, and her love for Jack Daniel's, she doesn't realize who he is. Richard D. Laudenslager, author of *Wounded,* says, "KUDZU RIVER is to Fran Rizer's previous cozy books what a great white shark is to a guppy."

The HORROR of JULIE BATES

Who knew Columbia, South Carolina, could be so scary?

Preface from Fran Rizer:

When a red-haired woman approached me at a book-signing, I expected her to ask me to autograph one of my cozy mysteries. Instead, she asked me to write a book for her. I went into my usual spiel that she could do a better job of putting her story on paper than I would, but we agreed to meet in the coffee shop after the signing. Writers are frequently approached to write or co-write someone else's story. Most of the time, we decline politely, but there was something about her that made me hesitate to dismiss her so quickly.

The HORROR of JULIE BATES is that woman's story. I spent many, many hours recording Julie Bates's tale and even more days and nights scaring myself as I wrote her story from her point of view. The occasional third-person chapters were added after I was fortunate enough to obtain Richard Arthur's journal.

Move over Amityville. Columbia, SC, is right beside you on the scale of terror.

First Print Edition September 2017

Cover design by David Smoak Graphic Design.

ISBN – 13: 978-0692901885
ISBN – 10: 9692901884

A SKULL
FULL OF POSIES

Fran Rizer

Dedicated to the Memory of

My Parents

Frances Willene Baker Gates

and

Everett Clyde Gates

Saturday, October 24

Chapter One

"NOTHING LIKE A DIVORCE to leave a person commitment-shy," Sheriff Wayne Harmon says as we talk by phone while I drive to the Halsey place. To be honest, and I try to be, I've had enough (actually, too much) of this conversation for the past few weeks, and if I weren't trying to be more of a lady, I would do the cell phone equivalent of hanging up on him. I miss the old days before everyone had a cell because simply disconnecting doesn't have nearly the pow factor of slamming down the telephone receiver.

I'm not happy to be heading toward the Halsey property this Saturday morning anyway, but this particular commitment is my own fault.

Tyrone, my friend Rizzie Profit's teenaged brother, called me at work a few days ago and asked could I "get" him a real casket for the haunted house his TEAM class planned to sponsor for St. Mary High School's Fall Festival (aka Halloween carnival). TEAM classes are an instructional program teaching leadership and cooperation through community projects and fund-raising.

"Ty," I said, "caskets cost thousands of dollars, and I'm sorry, but I can't afford to buy one for you even with the discount Otis and Odell Middleton would allow me."

"Callie, I don't want you to 'give' us one. I told my friends that since you work at the funeral home, the Middletons might *lend* us a casket."

"We can't do that because the law forbids us from selling a used casket, so it wouldn't do us any good to get it back."

"We won't put a real corpse in it," he said.

"I should hope not, but legally it would still be considered secondhand."

"Oh." The disappointment I heard in Ty's voice put me on a guilt trip. I pictured him bragging to his friends that he could get a real casket for their project. I should have apologized for not being able to help at all and let it go at that.

Instead, my mouth flew open and out came, "Tell you what, Ty. I'll find something for you to use for a coffin, and I'll volunteer to help set up the haunted house." That's how I wound up driving out to the Halsey house on a cool Saturday morning in October arguing with my current paramour (same thing as a boyfriend except I'm a little past thirty, and "boyfriend" sounds sixth-gradish to me). I've known Sheriff Wayne Harmon since I was a little girl, and he's my oldest brother John's best buddy. Through the years, he became a friend of mine and recently our relationship moved up to a higher level— much, much higher—or perhaps a lower level in some folks' opinion.

Wayne is headed back to St. Mary from Virginia where he attended a six-week-long FBI Academy Seminar. He sees no reason why I don't just donate a healthy check to the TEAM project and spend the day with him when he gets back to town. We have plans to attend his twenty-seventh high school reunion tonight. He volunteered to supply the contribution and even talked to the Middletons to be sure I had the whole day off this Saturday. He also can't understand why I won't agree to marry him. Don't get me wrong. I love the man. I don't want to lose him, but I'm not ready to marry him.

Neither Wayne nor I have a great record when it comes to marriage. I've been divorced once, and Wayne has two behind him.

I'm not about to claim I've never told a lie to a man. If I say that, lightning will probably come down from the perfectly clear, crisp morning sky and strike me dead. Or hit my new car. My 1966 Mustang was my ex-husband's pride and joy before the judge gave it to me in divorce court, but my new creamy yellow Corvette is now my most prized possession and eases the pain of losing the Mustang. Don't misunderstand. My Vette is one of the cheapest models, but it's new, and I didn't mind financing it for what's going to seem like forever.

What I can say is that I've never broken a promise to a child, and though Ty looks like a man, he's still a kid to me.

Confession is supposed to be good for the soul, so I'll admit that all those thoughts about Tyrone, Wayne, and my car are just ways to escape thinking about the fact that I'm headed to the Halsey place. I almost passed out when Tyrone told me the bank foreclosed on that property and since one of his classmates is the bank president's daughter, the TEAM class has been given use of the old house. That place is the home of many of my worst thoughts and memories.

They couldn't choose a worse place for me personally. My Mustang died in the woods behind that house when my brother Bill crashed it into a tree. Several years earlier, I came close to dying there myself when a killer kidnapped me and locked me in the barn. Worst thing about it was that I was in a stolen, sealed casket. I was rescued by my current sweetheart, Sheriff Wayne Harmon.

The Halsey property is wooded behind the pasture and barn, but the long driveway from the road to the old farmhouse in front is typical coastal South Carolina. Oak trees draped in

Spanish moss line both sides of the road. Just beyond the trees are abandoned fields that were farmed in the past, probably cantaloupe, cucumbers, or tomatoes.

The two-story building at the end of the driveway isn't a Southern mansion with a veranda, big white columns, or a balcony. The front of the house is flat except for a small porch that sticks out from the exterior wall. It gives me the heebie-jeebies, not because of its looks, but because of my associations with this place.

Near the path leading up to the front door I see a blue passenger van. A grown man and six teenagers including Ty stand beside it. They all gather around my Vette the minute I park.

Ty holds my car door open for me and says, "Everybody, this is Callie Parrish, our volunteer. She's gonna be a lot of help because she works at Middleton's Mortuary." He points toward the only adult male and adds, "Callie, this is Mr. Douglas, our teacher."

"Glad to meet you, Ms. Parrish. We appreciate your offer to help." The instructor motions toward the steps. I glance over and notice that some of them have been repaired with new boards.

Mr. Douglas must notice where I'm looking because he says, "I came out earlier this week and saw some wood that didn't look safe, so I replaced it, but I want everyone to be especially careful.

Let's go in and look around. We can decide what to put where."

He opens the door and holds it for me with the students behind us. We enter a hall with closed doors and on the left side, there's a stairway leading to the second floor.

"Let's start upstairs," I say and begin climbing up.

The next thing I hear is a loud scream. It comes from me. The next thing after that, I feel skin tearing as I crash through a rotten step. I grab the stair above and stop my fall with the top half of my body sticking out of the hole in the wood. From my armpits on down, I'm suspended over whatever is beneath the stairway.

I don't know who reaches me first because Tyrone grabs one arm just as fast as Mr. Douglas snatches the other one. They attempt to pull me upright, but my perky behind catches against the splintered step.

"I think our best bet is to enlarge the opening enough to pull her out. Tyrone, can you hold her up while I go to the van for a tool?" Mr. Douglas says.

Ty nods, moves up to the next step, and turns around to face me. Holding on to the arm he first grabbed, he grasps my other wrist, the one Mr. Douglas is holding. Mr. Douglas lets go and starts down the steps.

Just then it happens. I'm so surprised that for a moment, I don't grasp the situation.

Squatting on the step above me, Ty loses his balance.

He drops me.

I fall on my back and land on a hard surface below the stairwell. It's not a long plunge, but it knocks the breath out of me. I can hear the kids upstairs yelling for Mr. Douglas while Tyrone calls my name as he wiggles and squirms his way through the hole and down to my side.

"What in the (not a kindergarten cuss word) is this?" he asks.

I sit up and Ty gives me a gentle shove back down to my back.

"Don't move," he says, "until we know how bad you're hurt."

"I'm sure I have a few scrapes through my shirt, but everything seems to be working." I wiggle my hands and feet.

Ty asks, "How about your neck, your head, your back?"

"All okay," I say, look up, and roll my neck like some women do when they're irritated—the motion that goes with eye rolling.

When I move my head, I see what Tyrone saw when he lowered himself down beside me. I twist myself over to a sitting position and get a better look.

The room is small, only the width of the stairway above. The ceiling, slanted from about ten or twelve feet high on one end, slopes to a very acute angle on the other. Directly in the middle, a little nearer the highest part of the ceiling than where I fell is a bushel basket flipped upside down with the open end against the unfinished wooden floor.

In the darkness of the enclosed space with no windows, what sits on the upended basket at first appears to be a white pumpkin surrounded by red flowers. Focusing harder, I see that the flowers surround not a pumpkin but a skull and that the flowers seem fresh. On second glance, I realize they don't look wilted because they're artificial.

"Looks like somebody's already started decorating for Halloween," I say.

"That's not funny," Ty snaps. "There's a little door in this wall. Let's get out of here."

He looks up where Mr. Douglas is attempting to widen the hole with a saw. "Hold on," Ty calls. "There's a door down here. We'll see where it leads. Okay?"

Of course, when Ty says, "little door," I think of *Alice in Wonderland*—that table where she found the food and drink that made her grow and then shrink to mouse-size. This door isn't that small. It's shorter than I am though, and I'm five feet, four inches tall. I'll have to duck down low or crawl to get out through there.

Ty helps me from the floor, but unless I go closer to the end of the room, I can't stand up all the way. We both hunch over to stand near that small door. It has a glass knob. Ty turns it, and the door opens. I confess I'm holding my breath, scared of what we might find.

Squeals of teenaged joy welcome us. The other students stand in the entrance hall on the opposite side of the door, gathered at the foot of the stairs just a couple of feet from the undersized door. A boy with a long, dark ponytail extends his hand to me as I creep out of the room and into the hall. He's wearing baggy black jeans and a black, saggy sweatshirt.

"I'm Raven. Let me help you."

"His name's not Raven. It's Zack. He just likes to call himself Raven," Ty says.

"I believe a person can call himself whatever he likes," I say. "I call myself Callie and I sure like that better than Calamine."

Raven/Zack grins.

Mr. Douglas joins us, apologizing for not replacing the step I fell through.

"Thank heaven that room or closet is beneath the stairwell," he says. "Otherwise you might have fallen all the way through to the crawl space beneath the house."

"Mr. Douglas," Ty interrupts, "I think you should take a look at what's in that room. Did you set up a fake skull planning to take us in there and scare us?"

The guy who helped me asks, "What? What is it?"

"There's a skull in there, Zack," Tyrone says. I can hear fear in his voice.

"I didn't even know that room existed. I'll check it out." Mr. Douglas pulls the door open wider, stoops, and enters. After only a minute, he steps out with his cell phone in hand. "I'm calling the sheriff," he says.

"He's out of town," I tell the teacher.

"Then 911 will send a deputy. That's not a Halloween skull in there. It's the real thing—a human skull on the basket and several other bones lying under a burlap sack in the corner." He frowns. "I want all of you outside. Tyrone, you get the first aid kit and see if you can clean Ms. Parrish's cuts. Bandage them until we get her to a physician."

"I don't believe I need a doctor," I say.

"We don't know what that is beneath the stairs, and you have open abrasions on your arms there." He points at a scrape. "I insist that you go directly to the emergency room." He looks around. "Are you willing to let Tyrone drive you there in your car?"

Zack jabs Ty in the ribs. "Did you knock Miss Parrish through the steps to get to drive her fancy car?"

Ty reacts with a frown and a gruff, "That's not funny, Zack. I'd never intentionally hurt Callie."

"Can Tyrone drive you to the ER?" Mr. Douglas asks me again.

I haven't let anyone drive my new car since I bought it—not even Wayne or Daddy, but I say, "Certainly."

Before Ty finishes bandaging, the deputy arrives, nods toward me, and asks, "Is she supposed to be a mummy for this haunted house?"

I laugh. "No. I have a very enthusiastic doctor here who's making sure every cut is covered."

Tyrone looks embarrassed and spins the Vette's tires as we leave. Maybe the deputy and I shouldn't have teased him; teenagers can be ultrasensitive.

My chauffeur slows down and smiles as he says, "I didn't bandage your booty. I bet it's scraped through your jeans because that's all that was holding you up between those broken boards."

"Don't worry about my behind," I say. "I'll guarantee there's not a scratch on it. I'm wearing my fanny panties."

"What's that?"

"There's a little padding back there that's built into my underwear instead of part of me."

"That's why the junk in your trunk is perkier some days than others?"

"How do you know that?"

"Callie, I'm growing up."

This is getting a bit embarrassing for me. I'm not comfortable talking about my tush nor my underwear with a teenaged boy. I change the subject. "Ty, do you have any idea what we saw back there under the steps? Was it some kind of Gullah thing?"

"I'm not sure, but it's bad. Whatever or whoever put those bones there wasn't doing anything
good."

Chapter Two

SAME OLD, SAME OLD at the ER, except Dr. Donald Walters isn't here. Like a bad penny, he usually shows up when I make an unexpected trip to the hospital. I shouldn't say *like a bad penny*. The doc has been a good friend though he wasn't very good boyfriend material. That doesn't matter now that I'm in an exclusive relationship with Sheriff Wayne Harmon.

"Nurse, please clean up these scrapes and abrasions." This new physician takes out his little flashlight and peers into my eyes. "Did you hit your head when you fell?" he asks.

"No, sir," I answer.

"Might as well get a brain CT anyway to be on the safe side and an X-ray of the rib cage to be sure nothing is broken and puncturing anything internally." He stops looking in my eyes and asks,

"When was your last tetanus shot?" I don't know why, but I suddenly wish he was Donald.

"I'm not sure," I reply.

"It's right here in her record," the nurse says. "She's a regular in emergency. Last tetanus was only six months ago."

"A frequent ER patient?" the doctor asks.

"I do tend to get into lots of scrapes and have lots of knocks on the head," I say.

"Who's the young man who brought you in?"

"My friend's younger brother." I pause. "Well, he's my friend, too. I was at the old Halsey place with his teacher and some of his classmates. They're turning the building into a haunted house for the carnival next weekend. I fell through a weak spot on the stairs."

"Are you sure you're not playing some kind of cougar game with that young kid? Did you make him mad and he put his hands on you?"

I laugh at the absurdity of his thinking I'm hooking up with Tyrone and at the thought Ty could inflict this much damage on me and not be wearing a few cuts and bruises himself.

"Do you think it's funny?" The doctor's face assumes a puzzled expression.

"No, I think it's ridiculous to even consider that."

WHEN THE TESTS are completed and I'm released, I feel well enough to drive, but I know

Tyrone wants to get behind the wheel of the Vette again, so I sit in the passenger seat after he pulls the car up to the ER door.

"Where to?" he asks.

"The grill," I answer, meaning the Gastric Gullah Grill owned by my friend, his sister Rizzie Profit.

"I could take you home to rest and be your driver for a few days," he suggests like he really believes I'm letting a seventeen-year-old take my new car out of my sight. It took all of my insurance money plus a loan that's more like a mortgage for a house than a car payment to get this beauty.

"Thanks, but no, thanks," I answer. The CT was negative—no sign of concussion, so I don't feel the need to fight off the urge to nap on the drive.

I awake to a gentle tap on the shoulder and Rizzie asking, "Callie? Callie? Wake up. Are you okay?"

"I'm fine, just tired."

"Come on inside. I want you to meet somebody."

When Rizzie first opened the grill, she wore traditional Gullah clothing—bright colorful African fabric wrapped around her body, sometimes as a skirt with a blouse, sometimes as a dress covering her from the top of her bosom to her ankles. She also wore head cloths that looked like turbans and occasionally spoke the Gullah language to impress tourists. The restaurant was decorated with original Gullah artwork and intricately woven sweetgrass baskets, one of the best-known Gullah handicrafts. As time passed and the restaurant demanded more and more of her time, she added more Gullah baskets and crafts to the restaurant décor but gradually stopped dressing African at work.

"We had a little accident at the haunted house," I begin to explain when Rizzie motions me to sit at a booth across from a man wearing khaki shorts and a golf shirt like one I saw on Charlie Harper in a rerun of *Two and a Half Men*. The man's blue eyes provide stark contrast with his deep golden tan and thick hair that's whiter than new-fallen snow, which we're lucky to get once a year here on the coast of South Carolina.

"I know, Ty called and told me about it." Rizzie places a tumbler of sweet iced tea in front of me and refills the man's glass before returning the pitcher to its designated place behind the counter.

"I want to ask you about something," I say when she returns and sits across from me beside the white-haired man, but Rizzie interrupts.

"Bob, this is my friend Callie Parrish." She's looking at the man as she motions toward me, and I can see affection in her eyes. Then she turns toward me and says, "Callie, meet my new friend, Bob Everett."

"Nice to meet you, Mr. Everett," I reply.

They both grin. "Bob, just call me Bob," he says. "From what Rizzie's told me, seeing her means I'll also be seeing a lot of you."

My expression is met by laughter from both of them. I gulp my tea.

"Bob is a retired archaeologist who moved to St. Mary to do research on this area, Gullah traditions, and Native American artifacts. We met when he came in and noticed the sweetgrass baskets and artwork." The only word to describe Rizzie's demeanor as she talks is "proud." Is she honored to be interviewed by a writer about her heritage and culture, or is something else going on?

Before I can think of how to ask a question that will explain her attitude, Bob excuses himself and goes behind the counter for the tea pitcher. He brings it over and refills my glass. Rizzie and I are close friends, but I don't go behind the counter in her restaurant, and I've never seen anyone other than an employee back there before. Then again, I've never seen Rizzie beaming like she is now either.

"Bob, would you mind calling Jane in here?" Rizzie asks.

"Certainly not," he replies and goes to the kitchen door at the end of the counter.

"Is Jane in your kitchen?" I ask.

"You've been so involved with the sheriff since you two hooked up that you haven't been around enough to keep up with what's going on." Rizzie grins even bigger. "Jane's working for me now. She's a wonderful cook, and so long as I don't forget and put something back in the wrong spot, she handles the kitchen as well or better than I do."

I'm not surprised by this. Jane Baker has been my best friend since her mom brought her home from the School for the Blind when we were in the ninth grade. She's a better cook than I can even dream of being—so long as everything stays in its assigned place. We learned that when Jane and I were roommates and I left the garlic powder where the cinnamon belonged.

"Did she quit her other job?" I ask.

"I don't know. So far as I'm concerned, that's a *don't ask, don't tell* situation. Tyrone usually brings her to work and takes her home, but I do know your brother Frankie has picked her up a few times when she said they were going out. Does that mean she's quit the other job? I don't know."

Frankie and Jane have an on-again, off-again relationship. I believe they love each other, but Frankie isn't my most reliable brother and doesn't keep a job very long at a time. Though he won't work and support her, he's violently opposed to Jane's job supporting herself as "Roxanne," whom she calls her "fantasy actress" persona. To call a spade a flippin' shovel, Roxanne is a telephone sex operator. Before Jane began doing that, her blindness made transportation to and from work a problem. Being Roxanne enables her to work from home, and the hours are flexible. Oops! I described Frankie as *violently* opposed. Too strong. That's a misstatement. They argue, but he's never hit Jane or abused her in any physical way.

Thoughts of my brother Frankie's romance with my best friend Jane cease when my phone alerts me to a new email. I read:

Why . . . When you give someone your heart, and love them for who they are and you support them, help them, give them financial support when they need it and are always there for them when they need you do they LIE and CHEAT! They can't even have an adult conversation with you instead they have a temper tantrum, and hang up on you and all bc they are caught. We are adults, I never deserved this ever . . . I love him, I probably always will, but I'm deeply hurt bc I trusted him and I lost my best friend . . . His son I love very much and this makes it so much harder bc of kids . . . Honesty . . . is there any left . . . ???? Callie, please make him answer my calls

The email is from Madison, the divorcee my brother Mike has been dating. That's a big surprise because Mike is a warm, funny guy who adopted his first wife's six-year-old son, Tommy. When Mike's wife stepped out on him, Mike divorced her, but he requested visitation and pays child support for Tommy, who's ten now.

Madison's daughter Lacey is only a year older than Tommy, and the times I've seen them all at Daddy and Miss Ellen's for family gatherings, they seemed to get along fine. Unlike Frankie, Mike works full-time and though he likes to make up and sing risqué songs to aggravate me, he's a dependable kind of guy.

No time to ponder that email more. My thoughts are interrupted by Jane's voice.

"Callie, are you okay? They said you were hurt over at the Halsey house. I don't see why you'd even go there." Jane's expression combines concern and scolding.

"I'm fine. I fell through a rotten step and got scraped up some, but I'm okay."

"I've been wanting to talk to you. I get off at nine tonight. Do you want to pick me up?"

"I'd love to, but I can't tonight. We're going to Wayne's high school reunion. How about tomorrow?"

"We haven't had much time to visit since you and Wayne started seeing each other. I get off at nine so pick me up then tomorrow night, but right now I need to get back to the kitchen to have the dinner entrees ready on time."

I notice she hasn't brought her mobility cane, and Bob leads her back to the kitchen.

While he does that, I quickly ask Rizzie, "Is there more to you and Bob than talking about Native American and Gullah culture?" Really a silly question. I'm not stupid.

"Kind of. At first, he just asked me questions here, but the last few times, we've gone into town for a late dinner after I closed up the grill. Isn't he gorgeous?"

I check him out as he sits back down. Tall, slender, and moving with that fluid, but masculine ease like Dick Van Dyke in his elder years. Yes, I'll agree he's attractive—if you like old men. The guy's at least sixty years old, maybe seventy. Don't get me wrong. I like old men, but they don't put the sparkle in my eye that I'm seeing in Rizzie's.

That's not exactly fair. I'm twelve years younger than Wayne, but this Bob has to be twenty or thirty years older than Rizzie, and she has never had any problem attracting men. She's drop-dead gorgeous with a knock-out figure, long legs, and classic bone structure. Her skin is the color of Godiva chocolate, and her eyes are like obsidian. She's had lots of opportunities since I've known her, but Rizzie has been too busy opening the grill and making a go of it to get involved with anyone.

"What did you want to ask me about?" she asks when I neither acknowledge nor deny that Bob Everett is *gorgeous*.

"I met Ty's class and teacher at the old Halsey place to make plans to set it up as the haunted house for the Fall Festival next week. While we were there, I accidentally fell through a weak spot in the stairs."

"Outside steps?" Bob asks.

"No, inside, on the way to the second floor. Ty and I tumbled into a small room beneath the stairway. There was a basket down there, turned upside down. Paper poppies were scattered around a skull sitting on it. Wayne's out of town, but the deputy said the skull looks human. I was wondering if you know of any kind of Gullah traditions or voodoo connected to flowers around a skull."

"Traditions?" Rizzie demanded. "You're not talking about *traditions*. First off, if it's Gullah, we wouldn't call it voodoo. Maybe blue magic or root work, but not voodoo. Second, I've told you before that I've never practiced any of that, and I don't know anything about it."

"Well, the window frames and doors here at the grill and at your house are painted blue. That's Gullah, isn't it?"

"That's our culture. The blue paint on my windows and doors is just to keep away bad luck, like when you won't wash clothes on New Year's Day because it might wash away a family member by death during the coming year."

The anger in her voice surprises me. Rizzie seldom loses her temper or even displays emotions, "Why are you so touchy about this?" I ask.

"It just upsets me. Sometimes I wonder if Maum fell and died because someone put a root hex on her." She bursts into sobs as Bob puts his arm around her shoulder and then pulls her head against his chest.

"Why would anyone put a spell on Maum?" I ask. "She was one of the sweetest, dearest ladies I've ever known."

Rizzie lifts her head and looks at me through tear-filled eyes. Bob pulls several napkins from the dispenser on the table and tenderly wipes Rizzie's face. No need to ask Rizzie any more questions about her and Bob.

"May I interrupt?" Bob asks. I notice his voice is comforting. I nod. "Rizzie and I have talked about this, Callie. She feels guilty that the grill was becoming successful and her grandmother was working here when she fell. She thinks perhaps someone was jealous and put a mojo on Maum or the spell could have been on Rizzie with Maum's resulting death because the root worker knew that hurting Maum would be the most painful thing to do to Rizzie."

"Oh, Rizzie," I try to console. "That's just plain impossible. Why would you think anyone had it in for you or Maum? Stuff happens. Maum falling was an accident, and you don't need to feel any responsibility. Working here with you made Maum's last days a joy, and she was very proud of your success." I don't know what else to say, so I change the subject. "Bob, do you have any thoughts about the skull and flowers?"

He smiles, but it's a serious smile. "In my research, I read about a headless body found in these parts back in the seventies. It was never identified, but there was some question about whether it could have been involved with voodoo or root work. Another thing is that when they excavated some Indian burial grounds near Murrells Inlet, they found skulls full of Spanish beads." He pats Rizzie on her shoulder and adds, "I'll do some research on it."

A lot of questions race through my mind as he talks, but before he finishes, Tina Turner jumps from my purse. Not literally, of course, but she's the new ringtone on my cell phone. "What's Love Got to Do with It?" is my favorite old song of hers, but Wayne is a big believer in romance, and it irritated him to hear that every time anyone called me, so I changed it to "Proud Mary."

I expect the caller to be Wayne. One of the deputies probably called to tell him I've been involved in finding another body, though this time it's far less than a whole person. Instead, it's Odell, one of my bosses at Middleton's Mortuary.

"Callie?" he mutters. Odell Middleton has this grumbly, raspy voice, so I can always tell him from his brother Otis. "Where are you?"

"At the grill."

"Thought you got off today to do volunteer work for Tyrone Profit's class."

"I did, but now I'm at Rizzie's."

"Good. The weatherman is calling for rain, and we have a three o'clock graveside service at Taylor's Cemetery."

"Oh, no," I interrupt. "I can't work an interment today. Wayne's coming back in from Virginia, and his high school reunion is tonight. I need to go home and get ready."

"I'm not asking you to work the service. The regular crew I would have sent over there to set up are all out sick. I've got a substitute crew. All I want is for you to go by and check that everything's done correctly. You should be out of there no later than one-thirty or two o'clock."

"Do I have to come in to the mortuary after I go to Taylor's?"

"No, you can go on home since the cemetery is between the grill and your apartment. If anything is wrong that you can't have them correct or if they've forgotten something, call me."

A quick explanation to Rizzie and Bob, and I'm soon wheeling down the road toward Taylor's Cemetery. I broke my ex-husband's heart when I got the '66 Mustang in our divorce. I now understand how he felt. This creamy yellow Corvette is like having a baby. Not that I really know since I have no children, but I feel like I own the world when I drive it.

I take the time to call Mike. I never text while driving, but I have Bluetooth in my car and don't have to hold the telephone, so I don't mind calling.

"Yell-o," Mike answers. Of all five of my brothers, Mike is the silliest. He makes up funny songs and answers the phone with weird words.

"What's going on with you and Madison?" I ask without even identifying myself. He knows my voice.

"You talking about all that stuff on Facebook?" he asks.

"I haven't seen Facebook. She sent me an email."

"She's flipped out, gone off her rocker."

"What brought it on?" I ask.

"She mentioned wedding plans and when I told her I don't want to get married or live together, she went psycho on me. Check out her Facebook page when you get a chance."

"Did you ask her to marry you during some sentimental moment?"

"What have I said about marrying *anybody* since my divorce?"

"That you'd never try it again."

"The only marriage I know that's working out is Pa and Miss Ellen, and they're always gone on those cruises she likes, so I don't see enough of them to know if they are as happy as they seem or if it's put-on for Frankie and me since we're both living here at the house."

"When are they due back from Alaska?"

"The second week of November."

"Thank heavens."

"Why?"

"Because I don't want anybody expecting me to cook Thanksgiving dinner." Mike explodes in a big belly laugh. He's eaten my cooking.

26

Chapter Three

HELPING SET UP the folding chairs under the Middleton's Mortuary canvas awning isn't part of my usual work responsibilities. Checking that everything is ready for an afternoon service at Taylor's Cemetery isn't part of my job either, but I don't argue with doing whatever my bosses Otis and Odell Middleton tell me to do. I'm helping the guys out, determined to get away in time to do all the girly things to fancy myself up for Wayne's high school reunion tonight.

I can't leave until the part-time workers complete the preparations, so to speed up the process and get away as soon as possible, I begin lining the chairs in neat rows facing the open grave while the men install the equipment that will lower the casket. We need to hurry because the dark clouds overhead tell a country girl like me that they'll spill rain on us soon.

When the chairs are ready, I sit in one of them and look around, appreciating the mix of gravestones. Modern cemeteries have a neat appearance with the precise rows of bronze vases sprouting bright, artificial flowers, but I like the aged upright monuments. Taylor's is one of the oldest graveyards on the coast of South Carolina, and survivors are allowed to mark graves however they like—whether it's a flat metal rectangle, granite obelisk, or a twelve-feet-tall statue.

A grave commemorated with a marble angel about five feet tall catches my eye. It's a child-like winged figure with her arms extended as though she's standing guard over the grave, protecting the person buried there. It's not the angel that attracts me but the woman standing beside it. She's slimmer than I am, but about my height. Nothing unusual about that, but her hair is that bright carrot-orange color that even I, a beautician, can't quite match out of a bottle. The woman doesn't notice me watching her. She just stands there staring at the burial site in front of her.

"Callie," one of the workers calls to me. "We're done here. You don't see anything wrong, do you? Mr. Middleton said you'd be checking everything out."

I laugh and look around. "Looks fine to me," I answer. "Of course, you never can tell about Odell."

"Is it okay to tell him you approved everything before we left?"

"Sure."

I watch the two men load the mortuary work van, sliding shovels inside, probably thankful that excavators dig those six-feet-deep holes now. These days, shovels are used only to even out dirt where necessary.

As they drive away, the rain begins. The same old upright grave markers that make Taylor's so interesting make it look spooky under the dark clouds and with the trees bare of leaves that have fallen as winter approaches. Either the wind blew them out of the cemetery or groundskeepers cleaned them all away.

I look across at the red-haired woman again. She has no umbrella and is making no effort to leave or to cover her head. That's not the smartest observation I've ever made. I don't see a purse or anything in her hands or on the ground that she could use to protect herself from the rain. I dash to my car and grab one of the big umbrellas Middleton's Mortuary supplies for funerals. I keep one in my car, but my bosses know it and don't care. As I open it, I head over to the woman.

She doesn't notice me until I tap her on the shoulder and invite her to share the umbrella.

"I'm Callie Parrish. I work for Middleton's Mortuary and thought you might like an escort with an umbrella to walk you back to your car." I look around, but I don't see a single vehicle except my own on the curving roadway through Taylor's.

"What did you say your name is?" she asks.

"Callie, Callie Parrish," I answer.

"For a moment, I thought you said *Allie*."

"Nope, it's Callie. Well, actually it's Calamine Lotion Parrish, but everyone calls me Callie except my daddy."

"Your middle name is *Lotion?* How did you wind up with that?"

"My mother died when I was born. Daddy had five sons, but he'd never named a female baby before. All he could think of was pink. He named me Calamine Lotion Parrish."

"I'll bet you get lots of attention when you have to fill out forms. My middle name is Lara, spelled without the *u*. Smart-aleck clerks always tell me I've misspelled my name." She smiles for the first time.

"I'm Alice Patterson," she adds and reaches for a handshake. "Josie here is my younger sister. She always called me Allie." She motions down at the base of the stone angel where engraved cherubs fly around the name *Josephine Colleen Patterson* with dates that show she died twenty-seven years ago after only seven years of life. Below the numerals are the words: *Gone far too soon.*

I work at a funeral home but I'm still bumfuzzled sometimes about what to say to people who've lost loved ones. Otis tells me a simple, "I'm sorry for your loss," is adequate, but to me, that's not always enough. The little girl died over twenty-five years ago, but the woman's grief is written all over her freckled face as if it was yesterday. Time doesn't heal that kind of pain.

"Josie is my baby sister." I notice she says "is," not "was." She pauses. "I was twelve years old when she was born. She was struck by a hit-and-run driver while riding her bicycle on a dirt road near my family's farm when she was almost seven. The son-of-a-bitch who hit her left Josie there, and she bled out, probably all afternoon. By the time my mother found her, Josie was dead."

"I'm so sorry," I whisper, meaning it sincerely. I'm the youngest child and have no sisters, but I know how I'd feel if one of my brothers died that way.

The woman's tears change to loud, gasping sobs and she begins shaking all over. I pat her shoulder (SOP for mortuary workers), and gently nudge her to walk toward the road. "Let's go to your car," I say, wondering where it is.

"I don't have one yet. I took a cab out here to visit Josie first, planning to rent a car back in town. Don't know what I was thinking. Guess I was so eager to come here that I wasn't thinking at all. Figured I'd call another cab to take me back, but I don't want to wait in the rain. Could you give me a lift to the car rental place?"

"No problem," I answer and guide her to my yellow Corvette. She gives it an appreciative glance. That pleases me because it's still new enough that my head blows up like a big old basketball when people are impressed with it.

On the way back to town, I ask, "So you don't live in St. Mary now?"

"No, I left to go to college in August after Josie died that June. I haven't been here in years."

I'd seen the two unused gravesites beside Josie's, and I put my foot in my mouth like I do too often. I ask, "You never came back to visit your parents?"

My question brings another gush of tears from Allie. "My mother fell totally apart when Josie was killed. She never recovered. In less than a year, my dad shot her and himself. I had them cremated. I spread their ashes over a field of wild-flowers on our farm. I haven't been back since then, but my twenty-seventh high school reunion is tonight, and I decided to come to that. I planned to visit the field where I spread Mama's and Daddy's ashes after going to Josie's grave, but I don't think I'll go anywhere else today in this rain, not even the reunion. Returning here was a mistake."

"Your high school reunion? At the St. Mary High School?"

"Yes, you'd think they would have it somewhere different, but not my classmates here in the big town of St. Mary." Her sarcastic tone matches the snarky expression on her face, and she shrugs.

"My boyfriend is on the reunion committee," I say. "They decided to have it in the gymnasium instead of renting a facility because they thought it would be nostalgic. I'll be there. I wish you'd change your mind and come."

"Your boyfriend? Who is he? Maybe I know him."

"Wayne Harmon. He's the county sheriff."

"I remember Wayne. He was a nice kid."

"Did you ever date him?"

"Never, and you need to get over any jealousy you have about those high school days. Wayne was one of the quiet ones who didn't date often. Of course, if he's the county sheriff now, all the divorced cheerleaders who wouldn't give him a second look back then will be all over him tonight."

I pull up in front of Enterprise car rentals. The rain has stopped, so I don't get out to walk her to the office door under the umbrella. "Do you want me to wait and be sure there's a car available?" I ask.

"No, thanks. I reserved one before I came." Allie reaches into her jeans pocket and pulls out rolled-up cash. "Can I pay you for the ride?" she asks.

"Don't even consider it," I reply, "but you're going to need a credit card to rent a car."

"No problem," she says and pulls a thick stack of plastic cards from a pocket on the other side. "I left my purse with my luggage at Ola Belle's Bed and Breakfast when I got to town."

"I wish you'd come tonight." I chuckle. "You can hold me back if I get irritated with some woman who thinks a county sheriff is a good catch."

"Is he?"

"What?"

"Is Wayne Harmon a good catch?"

"Except for when he gets called in when we're trying to spend time together."

"Maybe I'll go to the reunion. You might need someone to keep you company while the sheriff fights off those cheerleaders." She smiles and turns away.

"Bye, Alice," I call. "I'll look for you tonight."

"You can call me Allie," she says and walks toward Enterprise's door.

ON THE WAY HOME, I can't help comparing my first reaction to Wayne's inviting me to his high school reunion with the excitement I now feel. My ten-year high school reunion was a family picnic where it seemed everyone but me was escorted by a husband helping with their two and a half kids. Not the most exciting or comfortable scene for me—a childless, dateless, recent divorcee. My first reaction to Wayne's telling me about his twenty-seventh reunion was dread, but the more excited he became, the more enthusiastic I grew. Allie's comment about the cheerleaders doesn't worry me at all.

I finger through my purse, remove the invitation, and take a quick look at it when I stop for a red light. In formal, Old English font, the graduates of twenty-seven years ago are invited to the Flash-Back Prom celebrating the year St. Mary High School opened—1959. My first reaction when Wayne told me the theme was to question, "Does that mean I have to find a skirt with a flannel poodle applique and wear socks with saddle oxford shoes?"

"No, it means we were able to locate old yearbooks. The first prom was held in the gym. We're having the reunion there and decorating it like the pictures of the first one. The theme is "A Night to Remember." So far as clothing is concerned, buy the nicest knockout dress you can find. I want everyone to see that I'm bringing the prettiest girl to the prom." His words made me wonder who he took to his real senior prom, but I didn't ask.

When I pull into the circular driveway at the brick duplex where I live next door to Jane, I park and walk around to the fenced backyard. My harlequin Great Dane dog, Big Boy, stays back there when I'm not home. The *big* in his name is totally apropos because he hits the scales at over a hundred and fifty pounds now, more than twenty pounds heavier than I am. I still keep him inside with me when I'm home, but when I'm out, he stays in the yard. He has a doghouse—

actually a ten-by-ten shed from Lowe's—for getting out of the rain, and he seems happy with his yard though he goes crazy with excitement every time I come home.

Today is certainly not an exception; Big Boy begins running around in circles the minute he sees me. A lot of training went into teaching him not to jump up on me when he grew so big he knocked me down. After he calms down, he comes over, sits in front of me, licks my hand, and follows me in the back door to the kitchen. He sits patiently beside the pantry until I bring out the bag of doggie treats. We shake hands, and I give him a treat. He follows me into my bedroom and lies down beside my bed.

I can't wait. I take the garment bag from the closet, unzip it, and hang the smashing purple dress on the back of my bedroom door. For a few minutes, I just stand there drinking in its beauty. I looked for a knockout dress for months, and the one I bought is a perfect fusion of sexy and sophisticated. The high neckline hides the fact that most of my cleavage comes from my inflatable bra, but the slit up the side of the skirt does nothing to hide my legs, which are my best feature. The new open-toed shoes are exactly the same shade of violet as my dress.

The next few hours fly by while I do all the "girly" things—long, soaking bath in imported bath oils followed by manicure, pedicure, and facial before I even begin on my hair and makeup.

I know lots of cosmetologists who prefer to have others perform these services, but I like to do them for myself. When I finally slip on the dress and check myself out in the mirror, I'm more than satisfied with the results. The time I spend cosmetizing (Funeraleze for making up) deceased people at the mortuary keeps my makeup skills sharp though I don't usually take the time to contour my own face.

Big Boy has to be banished to the backyard because he won't stop nuzzling the dress and licking my toes.

When I finish my hair and makeup, I slip on the dress, not worrying about smudges because I use mortuary makeup which doesn't smear nearly so much as regular cosmetics. I'm not into selfies, but I succumb to temptation and take a few photo shots on my iPhone. I'm kinda embarrassed to admit I'm admiring myself. I'm not much on Facebook either but I'm considering using one of these new pics for my profile picture when the doorbell rings.

Chapter Four

WAYNE'S REACTION TO MY DRESS is no less than mine to seeing him standing on the front porch wearing a tuxedo. *Dalmation!* I think, still using the kindergarten cussing I developed when I taught five-year-olds before moving back to St. Mary and the mortuary. I wonder what he'd say if I suggest skipping the reunion. He looks so yummy, and I haven't seen him for weeks while he's been in Virginia.

After he's inside and takes a breath from telling me how beautiful I look, he hands me the white box he's holding. Inside is the most gorgeous purple cattleya orchid corsage I've ever seen, and I realize that I probably was supposed to buy him a boutonniere.

"Will you put it on?" I ask and hand the corsage back to him.

"Doesn't pin," he says and shows me the elastic band on the bottom. It's my first ever wrist corsage. In the box I see a white boutonniere. I pick it up.

"Didn't know if you'd think of this," he says.

We grin at each other as I tell him, "Good, because I forgot." I pin it to his lapel and we're out the front door. "Do you want to take my car?" I ask when I see that he's driving his official sheriff's vehicle.

"No, I might get a call while we're there. Do you mind riding in the cruiser?"

The truth is that I would ride a mule to the school with him. I've known Wayne Harmon since I was a child. Seen him off and on all my life, and either talk with him or see him every day now that we're finally dating each other. Sometimes, when a woman sees a man so constantly, she forgets how good-looking he is. Seeing Wayne in the tux reminds me why I spent my early teenaged years with a gigantic crush on him.

The reunion decorating committee has taken turning the school gym into a ballroom seriously, but they stuck with the photos in the yearbook. What looks like miles of green and white crepe streamers run from each corner of the ceiling to a massive bouquet of white tissue flowers in the center. The flower-makers outdid themselves. Those flowers are everywhere—erupting from the basketball nets, centered in vases on each of the tables surrounding the outer edges of the giant room, and clustered along the edges of the refreshment tables. They've even attached them to the wall so they appear to be a floral necklace on the school mascot—a leaping fawn-colored cougar—painted on the far end of the gym.

Clothing ranges from those who took the 1959 date of the first prom seriously and are wearing fifties dresses with men in white sports coats and pink carnations to strapless gowns with mini-skirts. I even see one floor-length gown with a train. The woman wearing that dress also sports a tiara.

Wonder if any of Wayne's classmates are cougars and will show up with younger men? I think, but there's no time to mention that to Wayne because my brother John meets us at the door.

"Isn't this wonderful?" John asks Wayne. He glances at me and then steps back, takes a long exaggerated look, and gives out the loudest wolf whistle I've ever heard. "Wow, Callie! You look fantastic."

"Who'd you bring?" I ask.

"I came stag. I'm sure there will be at least one widow lady or divorcee who'll take pity on poor lonely me and let me have a dance."

Wayne points to the painted wildcat on the wall. "They'll all be cougars, John, looking for someone younger than you. Is that gray I see creeping out of your head?"

"Distinction, Mr. Sheriff. That gray just makes

me look sophisticated." He looks across my shoulder and adds, "Who is *that?*"

Walking toward us is a woman in red. Her shoes are red heels, definitely what my brothers would call "do me" shoes except that's my cleaned-up version of their term. I glance at John. He isn't looking at her shoes. What I produce with my inflatable bras, she shows in full flesh glory. One of Daddy's favorite songs is about a man who takes his prom date to meet his parents. The father says, "That's a cocktail waitress in a Dolly Parton wig," and the answering line is, "I know, Dad. Ain't she cool?" I think it was a Confederate Railroad song called "Trashy Women."

The woman in red isn't wearing a blond Dolly Parton wig, but she definitely has a Dolly Parton figure. All the important parts are on full display with deep waves and ringlets of dark auburn hair tumbling down her shoulders and brushing soft skin over firm flesh. The latest thing in wedding dresses is see-through panels over the midriff. This crimson-colored gown goes one-step further with cutouts showing bare skin. I think my brother John is going to have a heart attack when the woman walks straight up to us.

I swear I don't know she's Alice Lara Patterson until she speaks to me. There's no sign of a freckle on that face. "Hi, Callie."

"Good grief, Allie. I didn't recognize you."

"Surprising what a little hair color and

makeup can do, isn't it?" Allie flashes me a big smile and turns toward Wayne and John.

"Hello, Wayne," she says. "I think I would know you anyway, but Callie told me she's dating Wayne Harmon, Jade County Sheriff. How are you?"

"Hello," Wayne answers and adds, "I don't believe I know you."

"Of course, you do." She looks at John. "But I don't know *you*," she says.

"Oh, I apologize," I say. "This is my brother John."

"Johnny Parrish?" Allie's voice fills with surprise. "I remember now. Wayne and Johnny were best friends, and you were always kind to me. You both came to the service for Josie."

It's hard to say whether Wayne or John looks more embarrassed. Wayne speaks first, "You're Alice Patterson, aren't you?"

Allie nods.

"Don't feel bad about not recognizing me," John says. "I wouldn't have recognized you either. Your hair has darkened."

Allie winks at me. Apparently, her hair was that carrot-color I'd seen that afternoon when they were all in school.

An electronic screech and that idiotic tap some people make on a microphone interrupts John. The gym is filled with middle-aged former classmates decked out to impress each other with how well they're holding their looks. A bald-headed man who took the flashback senior prom theme seriously by wearing a powder blue tux with a ruffled shirt stands on the bandstand beating on the microphone.

"Ladies and gentlemen, on behalf of St. Mary High School, welcome back after twenty-seven years." He laughs. "Though I see some of you more frequently when you come for conferences about your children."

Someone in the audience yells, "I've got a grandson who is a student here now."

"You must have started in grade school." The bald man laughs.

The man who shouted explains, "My step-daughter's son."

"Who is that with the microphone?" Allie asks.

"Melvin Barnes. He was in our class, and he's the principal of the school now," Wayne says.

"How about you?" Allie asks, "Do you have children, Wayne?"

"Not yet. I'm divorced."

"That doesn't keep you from having children."

"I have two." John obviously wants into the conversation.

"Is your wife here, Johnny?" Allie asks.

"We're separated."

"Does that mean you'll ask me to dance when the band starts?"

"Definitely."

"I can't get over Mel being the principal of the school, but then he was the class president and voted 'most likely to succeed.' What about those other three he ran around with? They called themselves 'the four musketeers,' remember?"

"They all turned out fine except Fletch. Remember Fletcher Williams? He stays drunk most of the time. Lives down by Hidden Lake. I've heard he's drawing welfare and supplements it by digging and selling bait worms. A sad situation. Fletch was one of the smartest kids in school, but he never amounted to anything after we graduated."

"What about the others?" Allie asks.

John answers this time. "Norman Clark is chief of the fire department and Sam Blevins owns Sammy Bee's New and Used Cars."

"Well, I'll have to look Sammy up," Allie says. "I'm thinking of staying here in St. Mary for a while. It would make sense to buy a car instead of renting indefinitely." Allie looks around at the crowded room. "If you'll excuse me, I want to speak to some of the others."

After she walks away, John elbows Wayne. "Who would have ever thought little skinny Alice Patterson would wind up looking like that?"

Wayne smiles, but his answer is, "Seems a little overdone to me. She was a sweet girl, and now there's a hard edge."

"You never know what effect a tragedy like that will have." John turns toward me. "You wouldn't remember it, Callie. Alice's little sister was out on her bicycle and was struck by a hit-and-run driver. Later, after Alice went off to college, her dad shot her mother and himself. That gal's been through a lot."

"I met her over at Taylor's Cemetery looking at her little sister's grave," I say. "She's still torn up about it."

Fletcher Williams stumbles past us and accidentally bumps into me. He's made an attempt to dress for the occasion, but heaven knows where he got the raggedy pants and way-too-large jacket he wears. Obviously, Fletcher shaved for the occasion because he has cuts and nicks all over his face. The smell of alcohol surrounds him.

"Hey, Fletch, watch where you're going," Wayne says.

"Oh, sorry," Fletch says. "I didn't mean to knock into your wife here."

Wayne and John both laugh. John says, "That's not Wayne's wife, Fletch. He got divorced from Dee Dee. This is his date, my little sister Callie."

Confusion floods across Fletcher's face. "Little Callie Parrish? I didn't know she'd growed up already."

Wayne grins. "You may want to cut off the liquor for the rest of the night," he says. "I'd hate to have to take you to the jail to sleep it off on the night of our reunion."

"Yes, sir." Fletcher straightens up and pops his right hand up to give Wayne a brisk, military salute. "And, pretty lady," he adds, looking at me, "I hope I didn't hurt you."

"Not at all," I answer. "Not at all, Mr. Williams."

Fletcher blushes the color of a ripe, red, beefsteak tomato. "Fletch. Just call me Fletch."

As Fletcher staggers away, John asks, "Wayne, do you think it's safe to let him wander around like that?"

"I'll keep an eye on him," Wayne answers, "and I'll have the bartenders cut him off. He'll probably wind up passed out with his head on one of the tables, but if he keeps drinking, he could end up with alcohol poisoning. Come on. I'll take care of that now."

"Bartenders?" I ask as he leads me to the other side of the room where two young men stand behind a makeshift bar. "Are they serving alcohol here in the school?"

"Yes, bartenders. We got special licensing from the town council to serve beer and wine here this one night, but no hard liquor." Wayne leans over and speaks to the bartenders.

When he turns back to me, I ask, "Will there be a meal?"

"We considered having a catered dinner, but we decided on heavy finger foods. I'm sure the class of fifty-nine had little pimento cheese sandwiches, stuffed celery, and deviled eggs. We stuck with the finger food idea but lots of variety including my favorites—jumbo shrimp, sushi, and caviar pinwheels."

"I can't wait," I say as the band starts.

Wayne turns toward me. "We've never danced together, Callie. Could that be our song?"

We head toward other couples on the dance floor, and John joins a group of graduates standing around telling stories and laughing. From the dance floor, I can see Fletcher lurch toward the bar. He's arguing with a red-haired man and calling out, "I'm sorry, I'm sorry." Suddenly, he pitches forward and throws up on the floor, splattering bits of food on his and the other man's shoes.

The ginger grabs Fletcher up by his jacket lapel in a rough snatch. The principal runs over to them shouting, "Hush, hush. Shut up, Fletch," and the two of them manhandle Fletcher to the hall door.

"Who's the red-haired man?" I ask Wayne. I confess that what I've noticed during this fracas is that the man has what my friends and I used to call a "baseball butt." When I was in high school, some of us watched the Braves on TV not to follow the game but to check out the jaunty, firm-looking behinds the players showed in their uniforms.

"Norman Clark, fire chief. Norman, Melvin, Fletch, and Sammy Bee called themselves the four musketeers back in school. That's Sammy Bee catching up with them now."

"What does he do?" I ask.

"Sammy owns Sammy Bee's Auto Sales. I think I told you that earlier when we were talking to Alice Patterson."

"I believe you did. Do you need to go with them to take Fletcher out?"

"No, I imagine those guys have dealt with a drunk Fletch many times through the years. I'll let Melvin and his friends deal with him unless it erupts into a fight."

The band plays on and couples dance around the mess on the floor as Norman, Melvin, and Sammy lead Fletcher out into the hall. One of the bartenders comes from behind the bar with a cloth and wipes up the floor. A man wearing a custodian uniform brings out a bucket and mop. He scrubs that area of the floor and dries it with a towel.

"Want to get something to eat now?" Wayne asks.

"I'm going to the ladies' room. Then I'll meet you over by the food."

I make my way across the room, through the door, and into the hall toward the restrooms. A flash of red catches my eye, and I spot Allie leaning against the door to Principal Barnes's office.

"What'cha doing, Allie?" I ask.

"Oh, just headed for the restroom," she replies. We go down the hall together and into the teachers' lounge. It sounds ridiculous, but I've always wanted to use the teachers' lounge instead of the student restrooms at least one time.

"Are you having fun?" I ask Allie as we stand side by side touching up our makeup and hair.

"Yes," she answers. "I'm so glad I came. It's definitely worthwhile."

We go back into the gym, and Wayne leads me to the photo station—an overhead arch decorated with more tissue paper flowers and gold letters spelling out "A Night to Remember."

"That was the theme in 1959, wasn't it?" I ask Wayne.

"Yes. Wonder how many of those graduates still remember that night?"

"I'd bet most of the women do," I say.

When it's our turn to be photographed, we get silly and have our picture made with him holding me like we're dancing and doing a dip.

Around midnight, the party begins to wind down. Wayne and I are waltzing this time, and I'm pleased to discover he's an excellent dancer. Over his shoulder, I notice that Allie and Melvin are wrapped tight in each other's arms on the slow dances and showing off some dirty moves on the fast songs. An attractive, but definitely middle-aged lady wearing a powder blue satin dress that matches the principal's tux stands at the bar and glares at them.

"Look at that woman," I whisper to Wayne. "I wouldn't want to be on the other end of that look from her."

"Melvin better watch himself. That's his wife

Judy, and if she looked at me that way, I'd probably run."

"I'm thirsty, but I don't believe I want to go over there right now," I say.

"Oh, Judy won't bother us. She just doesn't like Melvin rubbing up so close to Alice." The song ends. "Come on, Callie. Let's get something to drink and see if we can distract Judy."

Before we reach her, Judy picks up her glass from the bar and hands it to the bartender for a refill. When he gives it back, she stomps over to Allie and Melvin. A quick flip of Judy's wrist and she's flung her drink into their faces.

Allie laughs. Melvin grabs Judy's wrist and dang near drags her to the door. Norman follows them. Sammy runs up to Allie and hands her a napkin to wipe her face. The music stops, and I hear Melvin tell Norman, "Get Judy out of here. Take her home. I have to stay until this is over and all the leftover beer and wine are off the premises." He looks at his wife with anger-filled eyes. "I can't believe you would humiliate me like this. You owe Alice and me an apology."

"I'm not sorry," Judy says, but she puts her hand in Sammy's and allows him to lead her out of the gym.

Allie walks over to me. "Are you okay?" I ask.

"A little wet, but I'll be fine." She giggles.

"Do you have a rental car or do you need a ride home?"

Allie laughs and says, "Don't worry about me.

I've got a ride home."

My words were more courtesy than a real question anyway. I assume she'll get back to the B & B the way she got here, and though I like Alice Lara Patterson, I don't think much of her rubbing all over Melvin.

When Allie heads toward another group, Wayne asks, "Ready to go? I've had about as much fun as I can stand, and I guarantee this has been a night to remember."

Chapter Five

I CANNOT TELL A LIE. Well, I can, but I try not to. Wayne and I don't always get along. Sometimes we argue, but that's normal for a couple. On the way home, he brings up marriage again. He starts bugging me for the umpteenth time that we need to either get married or live together at his house. I'm not ready for that yet, and my rib cage hurts. To be honest (and I just said that I try to be), I don't even want him to spend the night, though usually I like to sleep snuggled into his arms. The day has been too full. I want to sleep alone in my own room with my dog Big Boy on the rug beside my bed.

When Wayne parks in the circular drive in front of the duplex, I hop out and head to the fenced backyard to bring Big Boy inside.

My dog is not here.

My first thought is that one of my brothers has come by and put the dog inside. Wayne and I go into the apartment and search for the dog. No Big Boy.

We walk around the chain-link fence and check the shed Big Boy uses for a doghouse. Nothing. I burst into tears at the thought my dog has escaped from the pen and is lost. I'm not one of those girls who cry easily. I hate crying. I'm an ugly crier. My face turns red, and I lose my breath and gasp. Wayne hasn't seen me cry a lot, but he knows the only thing to help me is to wipe my face with a clean, damp washcloth.

We go into my apartment and, while he gets a cloth, I listen at the wall to see if I detect sounds of Jane next door. If she's awake, I'll ask her if she heard anything. Jane is visually handicapped. Well, the truth is she's blind, but I try to be politically correct, especially when talking about people's challenges.

All is silent. Wayne returns and gently wipes my tears away. I keep listening for some kind of sound from next door. Back in the days when Jane worked seven nights a week as Roxanne, 900 telephone "fantasy actress" as she calls herself, she stayed up all night and slept most of the day. Now that she's cooking for Rizzie during the day, I guess she's sleeping at night. Maybe she *has* given up the phone job. It would make my brother Frankie happy, but I don't know that Jane and Frankie will ever get back together whether she quits being Roxanne or not. Like the old song says, "Too much water under the bridge."

Wayne suggests we go for a drive and look for Big Boy.

After almost an hour of riding around with no luck, Wayne receives a call on his two-way radio. He tells dispatch, "I'll call you on the phone," stops the car, gets out, and makes the call turned away from me.

Back inside, he says, "We have to return to the school."

"Why?"

"There's trouble there."

"What kind of trouble?"

"They've found a body, but you're not going inside. You'll have to wait for me in the car."

No point in arguing, so I pout until we're back there and then begin quarreling with him. We don't fuss much, and I'm probably being the B-word because I'm upset about Big Boy.

"YOU WAIT HERE," Wayne says when he stops his cruiser by the curb in front of the school's main entrance. He jumps out of the driver's side while I open my door and step out, all the time disagreeing with him about whether or not I can go inside with him. I see my oldest brother John walking toward us.

"Don't be ridiculous. Who do you think Otis

and Odell will probably want to drive the body to Charleston for the autopsy?" I demand when Wayne insists I can't go in with him.

"Knowing the Middletons," Wayne replies, "I doubt seriously they'll ask you to transfer Melvin's body, and I personally don't want you to see it."

At least now I know whose body they've found. Wayne wouldn't tell me before. I wonder if the incident with Allie and the principal's wife triggered him to have a heart attack after the reunion ended. Wayne stands in front of me, holding his arms out with both palms facing me in a classic halting position as though he might shove me back inside the vehicle. I know better. Under no circumstances would Wayne ever push me. It's just a cop pose.

"I've dealt with all kinds of dead bodies," I snap back. John has reached the car and stands there listening.

"Could you just this once let me be your protector as well as your sheriff and the man who loves you?" Wayne's tone is much calmer than mine.

"Why?"

"Because I said so."

He says it like that should be enough for me, but it isn't. I close my car door behind me. I'm not a prissy little Miss Magnolia Mouth southern girl. Good grief! I work at a mortuary and deal with unpleasant deaths frequently. Wayne's words offend me even though he says them kindly. My brother John doesn't bother holding back the anger in his voice.

"For Pete's sake, Callie. Listen and do what you're told for a change. This is not something for you to see. The body is still hanging. Pa will kill all of us if we let you inside Melvin's office."

Hanging? That only makes me more determined, and I step forward as if to move around Wayne.

John, however, is my brother, not my lover. He's less likely to wind up in trouble if he "puts his hands" on me unless it's a violent contact, but he doesn't touch me. Instead, he says, "Follow me," and leads me into the school but in the opposite *direction* from where Wayne heads toward the principal's office.

John and I enter the school media center and head over to the computer section. He turns on a PC, and Googles something. I lean over and see: AUTO-EROTIC ASPHYXIA IS ONE OF THE GREATEST AND MOST DANGEROUS SEXUAL TABOOS.

The text continues:

Also known as hypoxyphilia, the practice is a sub-category of sexual masochism that involves reducing the oxygen supply to the brain while pleasuring one's self to achieve a heightened orgasm.

The Federal Bureau of Investigation estimates

there are between 500 and 1,000 such deaths in the United States annually, mostly among young men.

Many more may be falsely ruled as homicides or suicides.

"Are you telling me the principal pleasured himself to death in his office?" I ask John in disbelief.

"Technically, Melvin hanged himself. Can I trust you not to come creeping into the office if I leave you here?"

I'm a Google junkie, and I have no problem nodding my head in agreement. "I'll stay here and read more about this," I assure my brother. When I begin to read, I'm surprised that John has selected this entry for me. Daddy and all of my brothers except Mike tend to try to treat me like I'm still a little girl. They don't think I should ever drink a beer or have a glass of wine, and the only one who will tell an even slightly off-color joke to me is Mike.

I read:

AEA is practiced alone, which makes it particularly dangerous. The practice of limiting oxygen to the brain is used to intensify gratification. Strangulation, choking, suffocation, and other techniques to restrict breathing are used during this practice with a partner, but a frequent way when practiced alone is through self-hanging, which is the most common method among fatal cases. Though the deaths are sometimes ruled suicide, most are caused by accidents during the practice such as a stool being kicked over or unintentional tightening of the rope.

That's enough of that. I switch over to Facebook and check Madison Leonard's time-line. The most recent entry was eighteen minutes ago.

Madison Leonard
3:18 AM, October 24

When you love them for who they are and you support them, help them, plan a future for a family and are always there for them when they need you do they LIE and Why . . . When you give someone your heart CHEAT! They can't even have an adult conversation with you instead they have a temper tantrum, and hang up on you and all bc they are caught in their lies. We are adults, I never deserved this ever . . . I love him, I probably always will, but I'm deeply hurt bc I trusted him and I lost my best friend—His son I love very much and this makes it so much harder bc of kids . . . Honesty . . . is there any left . . . ????

This post is almost word for word what she emailed me earlier except for the request that I make Mike call her. I scroll back to see what Madison has said before then. Prior to ten days before, she was showing pictures of her, Mike, Tommy, and Lacey eating at Pizza Hut. She posted lots of memes about love and families. Then, all of a sudden, she's showing things about liars and broken promises.

"Miss Parrish."

Looking up, I see one of the younger deputies. I quickly sign off the computer.

"Sheriff Harmon asked me to drive you home," the deputy says. "He said tell you he'll probably be here most of the night."

I could sit there waiting until daylight, jumping from one Google article to another and reading Madison's Facebook page, but I don't bother to say that. The deputy leads me to the front door, looks out, and turns back to me.

"Let's find another way out of here," he says. The steps of the building are filled with reporters and photographers—both newspaper, television, and even a local radio DJ.

"Miss Parrish, Miss Parrish!" I hear one screaming. "Why are you here? Did you find the body? Please give us a statement."

A hundred and one dalmations! I think in kindergarten cussing. *It's not very nice to be known for finding corpses, usually murder victims' dead bodies.*

"Ignore him," the deputy advises, and we walk away from the door. As we pass the office, I see James Amick, the coroner heading in. "Did you come through all those reporters?" the deputy asks Amick.

"Better to go out through the gym or maybe the cafeteria door," the coroner answers.

The deputy and I head for the gym. The decorations haven't been taken down yet, but the festive air has dissipated. With the bright lights on, the green and white streamers sag. The balloons float lower from the ceiling. The floor is littered with green and white confetti as well as used cups and bits of napkins. Even the beautiful arch where we were photographed only a few hours earlier has lost its cheerful beauty.

Sunday, October 25

Chapter Six

TINA TURNER HAS FINISHED the dishes and pumping tane down in New Orleans before I hear her the next morning. She's rocking and rolling out of the cell phone on the bedside table and almost finished with the "nice and rough" part of "Proud Mary" before my mind wakes up enough to realize what I'm hearing.

The night before comes back to my thoughts in one big rush. I assume the caller is Wayne and that he'll tell me more about how Melvin Barnes died. From the article John had me read on Google, I assume that Melvin had some kinkiness I would never have suspected from the high school principal. That totally piques my curiosity to know details.

"Talk," I say into the phone.

"Did I wake you, Callie?" The young voice

catches me off guard.

"No, I was already awake, Tyrone," I lie.

"Mr. Douglas called and said the sheriff is keeping that yellow tape around the Halsey house and something happened at the school last night that's making them close the school for a week. The festival is this Saturday. Do you have any ideas about a place for our TEAM project?"

"Not really," I answer. Truth is that my mind is now fully awake, and I'm more concerned about Big Boy than I am about Ty's school project. I get out of bed and go to the back door while talking to Ty. I look out. Still no Big Boy.

"I'll be picking Jane up in about thirty minutes to come cook today's entrees. Rizzie is handling the breakfast crowd. Are you going to church or could you ride back to the grill with us and brainstorm with me? The TEAM class is meeting at two o'clock this afternoon, and I want to have some really good ideas to present."

"I'll brainstorm with you, but I'll drive myself over." I fight the sting of tears in my eyes as I add, "Big Boy is missing. I need to call animal rescue and see if they picked him up. After you and I meet, I'll go look for him some more."

"I'll help except for during the TEAM meeting." Ty pauses. "My teacher said to invite you to join us."

'We'll see," is my noncommittal answer. "I'll catch you at the grill."

Ty's call not only wakes me, it clues me in that

Jane is probably awake getting ready. I telephone her.

"How was the reunion?" Jane asks. "I'll bet you looked beautiful."

"I held my own, but a lot happened. I'll tell you about it later. I called about Big Boy."

"What about him?"

"When I got home last night, he wasn't in the yard. Wayne and I went looking for him, but we didn't find him. Did you see or hear anything at all from out back last night?"

It may seem strange that I ask totally blind Jane if she saw anything. When we first met, I was very careful not to ever use sight words, but I soon learned it doesn't bother her. She says, "See ya later," frequently. If she talks with someone and tells me about it, Jane will say, "I saw so and so at the mall today."

"No," she responds to my question. "Everything was normal. Will you still pick me up after work tonight? I want to discuss something with you."

"Sure. Nine o'clock. Right?"

"Yes, nine."

"I'll probably see you at Rizzie's in a little while. I'm going by there to talk with Ty about the Fall Festival.

"Then why is Ty taking me to work? I can just ride with you."

"I'm not headed straight over there. I want to drive around on the way and look for Big Boy."

We say goodbye and I head to the shower.

By the time I'm dressed and out the door, I
see Tyrone pull up in the van. We speak and I
put down the top of the Vette. The air is kind of
cool, but I think I'll be heard better calling for Big
Boy that way. I pull off and begin slowly driving
through the neighborhood calling out for Big Boy.
No luck.

I check a number on my iPhone and add it to
speed dial before calling.

"St. Mary Animal Rescue Center," the woman
answers.

"This is Callie Parrish. My dog is missing from
my fenced yard. He's a harlequin Great Dane,
which just means he's white with black spots. Do
you know if he's there?"

"No Great Danes here at all. Let me make a
note of your name and number. We'll call you if
anyone brings him in."

Driving around is no more helpful than the
woman at the rescue center was. No sign of Big
Boy.

A few minutes before I reach the Gastric
Gullah Grill, I call Wayne on his private cell
number.

"Good morning, sweetheart," he answers.

"Good morning to you, good morning to you,
good morning, dear Wayne, good morning to you,"
I sing to a tune close to, but not quite the same
as "Happy Birthday."

He laughs. "Did you get any sleep?"

"Yes, but now I'm out looking for Big Boy and then I'm going over to Rizzie's to help Ty with some ideas for his TEAM class's haunted house at the Fall Festival."

"I saw the skull my deputy brought from the Halsey place. Sent it off for analysis, but it looks genuine to me. Why didn't you tell me your rib cage was all scratched up last night? Did I hold you too tight when we danced?"

"It's fine—no worse than a skinned knee. Wanna join me at Rizzie's for breakfast or maybe meet somewhere for lunch?" I ask.

"I'd like that, but today looks too busy to make plans."

"Did Otis or Odell take Melvin Barnes to Middleton's? I'm asking because I'm working tomorrow and wonder if I'll be cosmetizing him."

Actually, I know perfectly well that as an unnatural death, the body will have to go to Charleston for an autopsy.

"No," Wayne responds, "we need to have a postmortem regardless of what Coroner Amick decides to call the death. The body went to Charleston for that last night."

"How did Amick call it?"

"He hasn't. He said it might be suicide, but I pointed out that I didn't think Melvin would commit suicide stark naked. Personally, I believe it was probably accidental."

"John had me read an article about auto-erotic asphyxia. Is that what happened?"

"We'll talk about it later." I know I've made him uncomfortable because he immediately says he has to get back to work. That's one of my problems with Wayne. He has a tendency to think he has to protect me like I'm still a child. I get that a lot from Daddy, too.

Business is slow when I enter the grill. A young couple sits in one of the booths, and Bob Everett is reading the newspaper in another one. Those are the only three customers. Ty stands behind the counter, and I don't see Jane or Rizzie.

"Hi, Callie," Tyrone calls, "How about a cup of coffee?"

"Sure," I answer.

He turns toward Bob Everett. "How about you, Mr. Everett? Need a refill?"

"Bring it on," Bob answers Ty and then says to me, "Come sit with me, Callie."

"I promised Ty I'd brainstorm the haunted house with him."

"It's okay," Ty says. "Mr. Everett has some ideas, too. Do you want me to put in an order for breakfast for you, Callie?"

"Yes," I answer. "I'm not sure what I want though. Let me think about it for a minute."

"Oh, don't bother thinking about it," Bob Everett comments. "Tell Rizzie to just duplicate my order. She's doing something special for me. You'll love it."

I slide into the seat across the table from Bob. "What's she fixing?" I ask, using that favorite

Southern word for preparing. Not that it matters. I've never known Rizzie or Jane to cook anything I didn't like. Of course, I may be prejudiced because while I don't suffer any inferiority issues about it, I acknowledge I may be the worst cook ever.

Before Bob answers, Ty brings my coffee and refills Bob's cup. He returns the carafe to the warmer behind the counter and then sits beside me.

"What's Rizzie cooking?" I ask again, waiting for an answer from either of them.

Just then Rizzie comes from the kitchen carrying a large tray. At the booth where we're sitting, she begins unloading. Eggs Benedict— one of my favorites. There are a few differences though. The Hollandaise sauce has little green specks, and there's no Canadian bacon sticking out from beneath the poached egg. On one side of the plate is a fan of bright red, sliced tomatoes; on the other side, crispy brown hash browns topped with bits of onion and cheese.

"Crab Benedict," Bob says, lifts his fork, and proceeds to take a bite.

"Yep, South Carolina blue crabmeat instead of Canadian bacon or ham," Rizzie adds.

"What's the green in the Hollandaise?" I ask.

"It's not Hollandaise. That's a bearnaise sauce," Bob answers the question I addressed to Rizzie.

"What's bearnaise?" I ask and take a bite.

67

Forget the questions. This is delicious.

"Tell Callie what bearnaise is," Rizzie says to Ty. "You want to become a chef. Show off what you're learning."

"Make fresh Hollandaise with egg yolks and melted butter, but add tarragon." Tyrone grins, and then asks Rizzie, "Right?"

Rizzie nods yes and says, "Between Jane and Ty, I should be able to make some time for myself away from the grill soon." She smiles at Bob and they exchange a look that is far more than proprietor-customer.

Rizzie heads back to the kitchen, stopping on the way to see if the other customers want anything.

I look at the table in front of Tyrone. No food. Just a Pepsi.

"You're not eating?" I ask.

"Ate before I went for Jane," he answers. "What's happening is this: Mr. Barnes died last night after the reunion was over. Mr. Douglas says school will be cancelled at least for a couple of days, maybe all week, in his memory. They've checked the projected weather forecast, and it should be fine next weekend, so the festival is being moved to the football field."

"What about the haunted house?" I ask between bites.

"That's what we'll be talking about. We were going to shuttle people from the school to the Halsey place in golf carts, but there's not another old house available to us."

Bob Everett takes a final bite of his breakfast, touches his lips with his napkin, and says, "Fresh activity is the only means of overcoming adversity."

"What does that mean?" Ty asks.

"It means that you defeat the negative by engaging in something new."

"That has to be a quote," I say. "Where's it from?"

"Those words are from Johann Wolfgang von Goethe, a German writer and statesman," Bob says, "but who they came from is not as important as the message. If you can't have a haunted house, think of something new, a fresh idea."

Tyrone looks at me and in complete sincerity asks, "Do you think the Middletons would let us have it in one of those big rooms at the funeral home?"

His question shocks me so much that I splutter coffee out of my mouth and across the table. The ultimate gentleman, Bob Everett smiles and wipes it up with a napkin.

"Of course not," I say. "The whole idea at Middleton's is to dignify death and help survivors through their time of sorrow. No way can there ever be something like a haunted house there."

The following ideas tossed into the conversation are just as unreasonable until Bob Everett exclaims, "I've got it! Not a haunted house but a haunted graveyard. All you'll need is a field, doesn't even have to be big. Make tombstones out of Styrofoam and coffins out of cardboard boxes—big ones like they have at appliance stores. Artificial flowers will finish the decorations. Then you kids can creep everyone out with scary ideas like having someone dressed in black with a scythe wandering around and caskets popping open."

"Zombies!" Tyrone's face lights up, and he begins calling his friends to run the idea by them.

I excuse myself, pay my tab, and set out riding around again looking for Big Boy. As I leave, Ty calls, "Mr. Douglas and the TEAM class are meeting at Ice Cream Dream, the place a block from the school, at two o'clock. Please try to come."

THE DAY SEEMS WASTED. I drive around calling for Big Boy with no response—don't even see any other dogs. I call Wayne, but he's too busy to talk. At half past one, I park behind Ice Cream Dream. Wayne is still too busy to talk to me, so I open Facebook on my iPhone to see if Madison has posted anything new aimed at Mike. Along with photos of dogs and cats, I see lots of cute things that make me laugh, but more than that, I see the political rants and people bemoaning their situations when I know from where I work that many lives are stricken much worse than those on Facebook. I admit that I used to be addicted to Facebook and other social media. Could hardly stand going more than thirty minutes without checking to see what was new. I made a conscious decision to wean myself away from those sites, and now here I am, eager to see what Madison has posted.

First, she's changed her profile picture. Madison is a pretty woman, but I notice that while certainly not in bad taste, in the new photo, she's wearing a low-cut dress and more makeup than usual. For some reason, she's put hearts above and below her post.

Madison Leonard
11:36 AM, October 25

No matter what I say or do its wrong . . . I have heard so many mean things towards me in the last 48 hours it's not right . . . Yet, I'm not the one that did anything wrong but care to much . . . Stupid me. I only asked for honesty . . . I don't care abt money, things etc . . . Yet this happens to me . . . I'm lied to, degraded and belittled and he can't admit what he was doing even when I busted his ass . . . I'm not dumb . . . Will delete all my fb pages tomorrow . . . anyone who contac info, IM me before 5 pm today. feeling sad

What did Mike do? Has he been creeping around? I call him, but the immediate answer is: "I'm sorry, but the person you've called has not set up a voice mail."

Now, I know that's a lie. I've left plenty of messages for him. He's disabled it. In only a minute, Mike returns my call.

"Hello," I say.

"Hello, darling," I hear in a perfect Conway Twitty imitation.

"What in the name of heaven did you do to Madison?" I ask.

"Told her I don't want to get married. She started pushing, and I told her maybe we need a break from each other. That made her ballistic and she's convinced herself that I've been cheating on her."

"Have you?"

"I swear to you that I haven't even looked at another female. You're talking to your brother Mike, not brother Bill. Madison was the sweetest woman I ever dated until now, but she's gone psycho."

"Did you ever propose or tell her marriage was in the future?"

"I told her when we started seeing each other that I never want to be married again."

I drop the subject and ask, "What happened to your phone?"

"Oh, Madison keeps texting me. Sending me these long, long texts that run ten and twelve inches. I've told her that I don't text when I'm at work. She doesn't believe I'm on duty today. For the last week, she's been stopping by the store, supposedly to ask me something, but it's to see if I'm here. When I told her it had to stop, I hurt her feelings. She's gone from bad to worse since then."

"Why are you working on a Sunday? Isn't that your usual day off?" I ask.

"K.B.'s sister-in-law had a baby yesterday. He took his wife to see her in Georgia."

Thinking about Madison's Facebook post, I ask, "Have you been calling her names?"

"Who? K.B.'s wife or sister-in-law?"

"Madison."

"I used to call her my honey, but today I did tell her she's crazy when she texted me all night insisting that the reason I didn't respond was because I was with someone else."

Ty parks beside me in the grill's van. I tell Mike I'll talk to him later and get out of the car.

"Glad you made it, Callie," Ty says. "You always have good ideas." I don't know if he's just buttering me up for more help, but it makes me feel good.

We walk into the ice cream parlor together and stop at the counter. I order a butterscotch milkshake and Tyrone gets a banana split. Mr. Douglas and three other teenagers including Zack are already discussing the Fall Festival when Ty and I pick up our treats and join them.

"The Jade County School Board has decided to keep the high school closed an entire week, so it won't reopen until the Monday after

Halloween." Mr. Douglas takes bites of his hot fudge sundae between phrases. The parent-teachers organization wants to have the festival anyway, and the location is going to be on the football field."

Tyrone speaks up. "I was going to suggest we have a haunted graveyard instead of a house."

"Great idea!" Zack says.

"But will they let us have enough space to do that?" Ty asks.

"That may be the perfect answer," Mr. Douglas says and wipes a drip of chocolate off his chin with a napkin. There's an empty field beyond the athletic parking lot. I'll see if we can use that."

The next hour is spent with the kids making a list of supplies they'll need. They begin with materials for signs and end with digging tools. Mr. Douglas tells the students to meet him at the football field Monday morning at ten o'clock. He invites me to join them, but I tell him I have to work Monday at Middletons. A quick goodbye and I'm back in my car.

Checking my email before I head out, I find three messages came from Madison while I was in Ice Cream Dream. The first says, "Callie, thank you for always being so kind to me and Lacey while Mike and I were dating. Please tell him to call me."

Second is: "Tell Mike to call me ASAP. It's important."

Last, she wrote, "Tell Mike he'd better call me

NOW or ELSE."

I drive over to K. B.'s Furniture. When I walk in, I see the other salesman, George, talking to a short, beer-bellied man and a woman I assume is his wife. The store is small, and the only three salesmen are the owner, George, and Mike. My brother is not in sight, and I wonder if he left, but he steps out from the back.

"Hey, Callie. I'm glad you stopped by. I have some great news for you," Mike says. "I want you to come out to Drew's Tavern Friday night. His bass player is out of town and Drew hired me to fill in for him." Mike has played with local bands before but not one as well known as the house band at Drew's Tavern.

"I'll try. If Wayne can't come, I'll try to line up a girls' night out with Jane and Rizzie."

"Awesome! What brings you by? Can I sell you a new couch?" We both laugh at that. Mike knows how far in debt my car put me.

"I was at Ice Cream Dream and decided since it's so close, I'd stop by to talk to you." I'm not eager to show him the emails, but I think I'd better. When I do, Mike's face turns bright pink and he explodes.

"She's gone loco and she's driving me crazy. I've told her over and over not to call me at work, but she keeps on. K. B. says no personal calls except for emergencies, so I haven't been responding, but she just keeps on and on and on." He coughs. "There were no red flags that she'd ever act like this."

"Maybe you two need to sit down with a mediator."

"If you're advising me to go to a counselor with her, I'm not doing that. She just needs to leave me alone."

I'm trying to think of something else to suggest when his face goes from pink to red and he steps around me headed for the front entrance. I turn. Madison stands there. She looks horrible. Her hair is a mess and her clothes are wrinkled.

"Get out!" Mike yells.

"You're going to talk to me," Madison says. "I demand an explanation. You sorry son of a (and she didn't say gun), you *owe* me that much."

"I don't owe you anything. I told you when we met that I don't plan to ever remarry. When you started pushing, I asked you nicely for a break— for time to think about our relationship. Who knows? At that time, I thought you were wonderful. If you'd agreed, we may have been back together by now, but you went berserk, and now I don't want to see you at all." He paused and looked around. "Where's Lacey? Isn't this her weekend home with you?"

"I can't deal with her right now. I took her to her daddy's house. I'm too upset, and now she's acting upset, too. She can't understand why you don't want to be her new daddy."

"I never said anything about being her new daddy, and I doubt she's disturbed about me.

Lacey is a smart child. She's confused because her mother is acting like an idiot."

If I've ever seen a woman move so fast before, I don't remember it. Madison shoots across the floor and slaps Mike on his face. It's a hard, loud blow. My brothers aren't known for great self-control, and for a moment, I'm scared. I don't know of any of them ever hitting a woman, but there's always a first time.

Mike steps back, moves away. He rubs his cheek.

George grabs Madison from the rear, wraps his arms around her. "You can't do that in here," he says. The customers he was talking with hurry out of the store. "I'm going to let you go now," George tells Madison. "You can leave the store or I'm calling 911 and reporting an assault."

Madison bursts into tears, but she walks out.

"Maybe you need a restraining order," I tell Mike.

"She'll calm down. Putting a restraining order on her would jeopardize her job as a police dispatcher." He gives me a hard look. "And don't you go telling the sheriff about this. I don't want to marry her, but I don't want to get her in trouble either."

I don't know what to say. To me, Madison is so far out of line that I'd want to take action, but Mike and I don't react to things the same way. He tends to deal with life on a more casual basis than I do. He jokes about most things and always sees the fun in everything, but Madison's actions disturb me.

FINALLY, I GO HOME to wait until time to pick up Jane. As I unlock the door, my stomach growls, and I realize that I haven't eaten a meal since breakfast. The Crab Benedict was filling and that milkshake was fine, but now they are gone. I check my cabinets and, as usual, find nothing but a box of Moon Pies. Not only have I not shopped for *food*, I don't have any Diet Cokes either.

Now, I love my Moon Pies, and some folks might say a Moon Pie goes good with anything, but there's no way I'm drinking water with my chocolate, graham cracker, marshmallow treat. I'm supposed to pick up Jane from work at nine, and I'm feeling sleepy. I put on a pot of coffee and settle on the couch to wait for it to brew.

As an adult, I understand that dating the sheriff means that sometimes he'll be tied up with work and unable to spend time with me, but it generally irritates me when it happens on a weekend. He was out of town for six weeks, and though he called frequently and we went to the reunion together, we haven't had any *real* time together in almost two months. Guess I'm feeling a little peeved about that when I pour my coffee and sit back down on the couch with it and not one, but two, Moon Pies. Yet I'm the one who didn't want him to spend Saturday night even before he was called back to the school. Mike has a problem with a woman who's too eager for commitment and marriage while his sister is scared to tie the knot again.

When Tina announces a call on my cell phone, I'm expecting—no, actually *hoping* that it's Wayne.

"Callie, this is Jane."

No need for her to say anything else. I know what's coming and her words are exactly what I expect.

"Can we get together tomorrow instead of after work tonight? Maybe for breakfast?"

"Well, Jane, the problem with that is I have to work tomorrow morning."

"I'll get up really early then. You see, Frankie keeps calling and pleading with me to talk to him. He said he's been going to counseling and wants us to start over. I gave in and agreed to let him pick me up from work tonight."

"Okay," I agree, but she can hear that I'm not happy with it. Jane and my brother Frankie were engaged for a while.

Jane's job as a 900 phone-sex operator seemed safe enough since the phone she used was a designated landline that was supposed to be untraceable. She and I were both scared to death when a phone stalker began calling her on her cell phone. When Frankie was caught as the stalker, he claimed he only did it to make her quit that kind of work. Since then, she's supposedly had nothing to do with him, and he has to attend counseling or be prosecuted for stalking. Guess I should be surprised she's talking with him again, but their relationship has been crazy up and down from the beginning.

"Don't be mad, Callie," Jane pleads.

"I'm not mad. I'm disappointed. Frankie is my brother and I love him, but after he pulled that stalker business, I wish you'd just stay away from him."

"Can we do breakfast tomorrow?"

"Knock on the wall when you get up, and if it's early enough, we'll have coffee together before I go to work. If not, I'll try to catch up with you later."

I disconnect the call and look down at the throw rug beside the couch. That's where Big Boy likes to lie when we watch television since he became too big to sit in my lap. I'm worried about him.

Nothing I want to watch is on television, and I get enough computer time at work posting obituaries. Besides, if I fire up my computer, I'll want to check my email or Facebook, and I really don't want to see anything about Madison and Mike. They're grown. Their problems belong to them, not me. I pull out an old DVD, and I'm deep into an episode of *Six Feet Under* when the doorbell rings.

I pick up my cell phone and walk to the door. "Who is it?" I shout with my finger on 911 speed dial.

"Wayne."

I peek through the bottom peephole and see that my sweetheart finally found time for me. I open the door and am met with a giant hug and a passionate kiss.

"Did you look out before you opened the door?" Wayne asks.

"Yes, and I'm glad you installed that second peephole." He added a lower opening when he realized that I'm too short to see out through the original one.

"Can you stay?" I ask, hoping the answer is *yes*.

"For a while. I came to tell you that Big Boy isn't the only missing dog in St. Mary. The St. Mary Animal Rescue Center reported that they've had six calls since last night from citizens whose dogs are missing from fenced yards. Chances are that the dogs, including yours, have been stolen."

"Stolen?"

"Yes, stolen. I've got a couple of deputies working on it."

"Are all of the missing dogs Great Danes?"

"No, I don't think there are even that many Great Danes in town. The missing dogs vary from a miniature dachshund to Big Boy."

"At least that's better than thinking he might have gotten out and been hit by a car on the road somewhere."

"That dog's big enough if he were hit, the

vehicle would have been damaged. Also, someone would have seen the carcass by the road."

"Don't call my dog a carcass." I think what upset me was the thought of Big Boy being dead, not the word *carcass,* though my bosses are adamant that I never refer to any of the deceased at work by the word *body.* We call the person by name or the word *decedent.*

"I checked your fence and I'm fairly certain Big Boy was stolen," Wayne says. "There's a dab of fluorescent paint on one of the posts. It's called 'tagging' and it means a scouter found your dog and marked your fence. Later, someone came back and took Big Boy."

I'm speechless, which doesn't happen often.

"Is that fresh coffee I'm smelling?" Wayne asks.

"Just made it. Want some?"

"Some what?"

"Coffee, though I wouldn't mind an overnight guest."

"I'll have some of both." He looks at the television. "Are you watching *Six Feet Under* again? Don't you get tired of death?"

"Come on, Wayne. It's like cop jokes. If you're in the business, you have to find some humor or you won't survive it."

"Well, let's watch something else. I've had enough mortality today."

"Did someone die besides Melvin Barnes?"

"No, that's the one. It's like you say about

cosmetizing. It's harder when it's someone you know—especially an old friend. I wasn't one of the four musketeers, but we all went through school together. I confess Melvin's death has gotten to me."

"Do you have the autopsy report yet?"

"Yes, cause of death—asphyxiation due to strangulation by nylon rope. Manner of death—suicide or accidental."

"Coroner Amick hasn't determined manner yet?"

"No, he's undecided. Wants to wait for the toxicology reports to see if Melvin had taken any kind of narcotics. Of course, we know the reports will show alcohol in his system. Everyone there saw him drinking, but then, most everyone else was drinking, too."

"Why did John show me that article about auto-erotic asphyxia? Was that involved?"

"It appears so, and if that's what it was, the death was accidental. I think that the coroner is trying to protect Melvin's wife and family, but either determination will be horrible for them. If Amick calls it accidental, people will wonder how he unintentionally hanged himself while others will guess the details. If it's labeled suicide, his wife is going to have some bad memories of that drink she threw in his face and maybe difficulties in collecting his life insurance."

"What do you think?"

"I think I love you more than you will ever

realize."

Wayne is a master at redirecting my thoughts. A wasted day turns into a wonderful night.

Monday, October 26

Chapter Seven

WAYNE AND I HAVE COFFEE at five the next morning. He apologizes for needing to get to work early and promises to call me sometime during the day. "I forgot to mention," he adds, "Alice Patterson called me yesterday. After I talked with her a few minutes, she wanted to know how to get in touch with you. I didn't think you'd mind, so I gave her your cell number."

"I don't mind. I like her. I think that red dress may have been some kind of statement she felt she needed to make, but I'll be glad to hear from her. I wonder what she and the principal talked about or did they just dance together Saturday night."

"Now, Callie," Wayne warns in his professional law enforcement voice, "don't go investigating. Melvin's death isn't a homicide and it's not your business."

"If the autopsy's completed, have you released the body?" I ask, thinking *I'm too upset about Big Boy to be thinking about investigating anything. I hope we never have another murder in St. Mary.*

"Yes, Melvin will be brought back to Middleton's here in St. Mary. Mrs. Barnes told me that she doesn't want a big production funeral."

"She wants it to be small and private?" I ask.

"Yes, but the newspaper is printing everything they find out, considering the circumstances."

"I wish you'd tell me all the circumstances."

"Keep on wishing. You're a cosmetologist, not a detective. Melvin's death is such a sad, unfortunate event for his family and the community. I have no intention of telling all the details to anyone."

I fake a pout which he kisses away and then leaves.

Crawling back into bed for a few more minutes of sleep, I try to mentally picture an accidental hanging. What would catch a person around the neck? If it was suicide, why and how? Wayne said Barnes died from asphyxiation by a nylon rope, but the high school principal had removed his clothes. That sure would fit with the Google article John showed me.

By the time I get up for real and dress for work, I realize that Jane hasn't called. A peek out the front window tells me why. Right behind my Vette in the driveway is Frankie's truck. It makes me want to cry, but I don't know if the tears would be sympathy for Jane knowing her relationship with my brother Frankie will probably be doomed again or if the tears would be anger at them both for their foolishness. I don't cry. Instead I take a shower, put on my big girl panties (the ones with the built-in perky tush), and go to work dressed as usual in the required modest black dress and low black heels.

On the way to Middleton's, I call St. Mary Animal Rescue Center again.

"No, ma'am, Ms. Parrish, we still have no Great Danes here." I should have expected that from what Wayne told me, but a gal has to keep hoping.

The stately two-story building that houses Middleton's Mortuary welcomes me as it always does. I love the columns out front, the white rocking chairs on the wrap-around verandah, and the large urns of flowering plants by the door. Huge old oak trees dripping Spanish moss from their gnarled limbs surround the parking area,

I escaped my now ex-husband and teaching five-year-olds in a kindergarten class a few years back to return to my hometown. After renewing the South Carolina State Cosmetology License I earned in high school voc ed, I went to work at a beauty parlor where the gossip and harping made me long for my students. That all changed when Otis Middleton, a town mortician and co-owner of the only funeral home, called to see if one of the cosmetologists could come over to Middleton's Mortuary and style a lady's hair because their usual stylist eloped the night before.

As the newest beautician at the shop, I was chosen to go to the funeral home. The rest is history. Odell Middleton offered me a full-time position as a cosmetician (not a typo, Funeraleze for cosmetologist) and girl Friday. As licensed morticians, both Otis and his twin brother Odell can do makeup and hair as well as preparation (Funeraleze for embalming), but neither of them likes to style women's hair. Suits me. I love doing hair for ladies who don't complain or want to gossip, and I enjoy making my male clients look their best, too. I've learned a lot from the Middletons, and they've adopted some of my ideas like Internet obituaries, memory videos, and selling unique items like gold lockets filled with cremation ashes.

I drive past the front of the building to the back where employees have assigned parking places near the loading dock. Behind the funeral home used to be as pretty as the front lot, but the addition of a warehouse for casket and supply storage changed that.

When I enter the back door, I smell something delicious. As usual on Mondays, Otis has brought in pastries. I go to our miniature kitchen and help myself to a sticky bun and another cup of coffee. Next stop is the office to see if either

Otis or Odell has left completed forms of obituary information to be entered on the computer. Nothing new, and I was all caught up Friday afternoon before I left work.

Otis and Odell were born identical twins, but time, habits, and diet have changed their looks. Otis is a trim vegetarian who had a tanning bed installed in the prep room—for himself, not our clients. Odell has about forty pounds on Otis, most of it in a protruding belly which here in the South might be thought to be a beer belly. Odell's comes from his addiction to barbecue instead of beer. When the brothers began to bald and Otis took himself to Charleston for hair implants, Odell began shaving his head. Buh-leeve me, their temperaments are as different as their looks except when they're dealing with the families and loved ones of decedents. Then they are both soft-spoken, consoling, and comforting.

I look around the kitchen area and out in the hall, but neither brother is visible. Back in my own little office, I fire up my computer and pull up our memorial pages. There's no obituary for Melvin Barnes. This probably means that Mrs. Barnes hasn't come in yet. Even though both Otis and Odell dislike computers, if an obituary is completed and I'm not here, one of them will post it.

Tempted to call Jane, I decide to wait. Frankie will probably be there half the day. Once again, he's unemployed, and from what I heard yesterday, Jane doesn't work breakfast hours at the grill.

Sometimes when I don't have a specific duty at work, I surf the computer. This morning, I decide to go back to my old ways and read instead. I reach into my bottom desk drawer and pull out a mystery by Agatha Christie. I've read it before, but I love her books enough to read them over and over.

"Callie?" I recognize Odell's voice.

"Yes, I'm here."

Odell opens my door and peeks in. "Mrs. Barnes will be here at eleven o'clock. I'll want you to sit in." Otis and Odell handle planning sessions, but sometimes they ask me to join them, especially if the situation is a difficult death with a wife or mother having to make the plans.

"No problem," I reply. "Is Melvin Barnes here yet?"

"Otis is on the way back from Charleston with him now."

I breathe a sigh of relief that I'm not being sent to pick him up from the morgue in Charleston where our autopsies and forensic exams are performed. I usually like being sent to and from there because I can ride along, thinking, singing, doing whatever I like in my mind. It's a secret, but sometimes when they send me to Charleston, I take a few minutes for myself and shop, but today I'm glad not to go.

The soft sound of an instrumental version of

"Blessed Assurance" sounds as the front door is opened. Both Odell and I meet Mrs. Barnes at the entrance. Today, instead of the powder blue satin, she wears a black pants suit that's certainly no match for Alice Patterson's red dress, but in her own soft, dignified way, Mrs. Barnes is as attractive on this Monday morning as Allie was Saturday night.

Odell leads us to the Camellia Room, which is a small conference room with a large gold-framed oil painting of multicolored camellias on the wall and a unique Asian vase with silk camellias centered on the round mahogany table. The four dark green upholstered chairs pulled up to the table have throw cushions made of a floral print fabric featuring camellias. The three of us sit at the table.

"Mrs. Barnes, this is Callie Parrish. She will assist us."

"I know you," Mrs. Barnes says to me. "Purple. You had on a beautiful purple dress, and you were with the sheriff at the high school."

"Yes, ma'am," I reply. "I'm sorry for your loss. Would you like some coffee?"

"I don't drink coffee."

"How about tea? I'll be glad to bring you some tea or a soda."

"I'd much rather just get this over with. I appreciate your kindness, but I want to be done with it."

"Yes, ma'am."

Odell places a clipboard in front of him and says, "First, we need to fill in the biographical details."

He asks Mrs. Barnes for Melvin's full name and other questions. The first time I went into a planning session with one of the Middletons, I assumed that I would serve as a secretary and record the answers. Not so. My job in a planning session is to sit quietly and carefully watch so that if the respondent becomes upset, I can comfort. I will also offer refreshments shortly after the session begins. I've already tried that earlier than usual, but I don't think it matters.

Mrs. Barnes patiently supplies Odell with information about her deceased husband, but when they reach the planning part, she says emphatically, "I want the shortest, simplest graveside service available."

"You understand that you are welcome to use our chapel if Mr. Barnes didn't have a church home," Odell tells her.

"We've been members of the same church for over twenty years, but I want only a graveside ceremony."

"Will there be a memorial service at the school prior to the interment service?" Odell asks.

"No, the School Board visited me yesterday and suggested that, but I declined." She takes a tissue from her purse. I expect her to wipe her eyes. Instead, she blows her nose. "Those idiots are closing the school for a week to show respect for Melvin, but I'm in charge of the funeral, and there is not to be any service or program other than a brief prayer before the casket is lowered. That man deserves no respect—none at all." Her eyes brim with tears, and I hand her a box of tissues from the side table. She doesn't bother to wipe the tears away as they trickle down her cheeks.

"Would you like some music?" Odell suggests. "We can supply a soloist or perhaps your church choir might sing."

Then I see it—the same expression Mrs. Barnes wore when she tossed that drink at her husband and Allie.

"I *told* you what I want. The children and I will ride to Taylor's Cemetery in my car, not one of your family cars. I do not want to follow a hearse, and there will be no pallbearers. You will have the casket positioned over the grave when we arrive. Someone will say a prayer, and we will leave you to your work. I want the barest thing possible. If you can think of anything less pretentious than that such as just sending you over there to dump him in the ground, let me know. The *only* reason I'm willing to do even this much is for my children's sake."

"Mrs. Barnes," Odell says, "I realize that the situation is difficult, but we have handled beautiful services for individuals who died in similar circumstances. The real purpose of visitations and funeral services is for the comfort of the survivors. You and your children are the ones to be considered here."

"You, Mr. Middleton, were not at the high school Saturday night when my husband of over twenty-five years made a fool of himself and embarrassed me beyond belief by drooling over that Alice Patterson woman, and I can't get a complete story of what happened after that, but I do know that his behavior was disgraceful and his death is scandalous no matter what the coroner decides to call it. Melvin is lucky that I'm burying him at all, and if he had any other relatives besides our children, I'd wash my hands of the entire proceedings." She stops and looks around as though wishing there were somewhere to hide in that tiny room with the camellias everywhere. "I don't want an obituary either," she continues. "There is to be nothing in the newspaper except what the reporters are already printing which hints at the outrageous."

"How about our Internet Memorial Page, Mrs. Barnes?" I ask. "Do you want just a simple statement of Mr. Barnes's survivors and the time and place of the graveside service?"

"I want *nothing*. Not in the papers and not on the Internet. The newspapers and local news can't get enough of writing and reporting about his death. I want him buried tomorrow during the day because tomorrow evening, my children and I are driving to the International Airport in Greenville and going to Europe for a few months.

We're not hanging around this town while everyone gossips."

Mrs. Barnes stands.

This is the first time I've ever seen Odell speechless.

As a paid employee, I think it's my responsibility to ask the questions related to my job of cosmetizing and dressing the decedent. "Do you wish Middleton's to supply burial clothing?" I ask though I'm pretty sure I know the answer.

"If you want to. I don't care if you bury him naked." She laughs. "In fact, that would be most appropriate, but you can dress him if you like."

"I'll select something," I say. "

"Do you wish to see Mr. Barnes before the casket is secured?" Odell asks.

"No, I don't want any part of it. I understand that I have to go to Taylor's and authorize opening the grave personally, or I would turn that over to you. I called them and they can be ready at three Tuesday afternoon if I sign the permission form before three o'clock today. Is that satisfactory with you?"

"Three is fine." Odell has a look I've never seen before, as though he can't believe what's happening. "If you're positive that all we are to do is be there with the casket ready for burial, I need you to sign this." He places the clipboard in front of her and hands her the pen. She scrawls something across the paper and turns toward the door.

"That's what I said, isn't it?" she snaps, turns, and walks out of the room.

"Amazing Grace" plays softly over the intercom, and Odell turns toward me.

"Otis and I will prepare Mr. Barnes. Select a nice suit for him, Callie."

I've had some strange experiences since I came to work at Middleton's, but this is one of the strangest. Mrs. Barnes is coming close to just abandoning the body like so many of those stories Otis likes to tell me about decedents left at funeral homes for years because nobody will pay the bill.

I go back to my office, close the door, and call Jane.

"Callie?" she answers.

"You sure are sleeping late," I say.

"Frankie is taking me to work, but we're getting something to eat first. Rizzie gave me the morning off. Can I call you back later?"

Fighting the urge to scold my best friend for her stupidity where my brother is concerned, I agree and end the call. Tina Turner immediately blasts out, and I think maybe Wayne is right. I should change that.

"Callie here, talk," I answer, expecting to hear Jane, calling right back because she's worried that she's upset me. Definitely not Jane's voice.

"Callie Parrish? This is Allie Patterson. I do hope it's all right that I got your number from the sheriff. Nowadays with everyone using cells, phone books don't exist."

"It's all right," I answer, not bothering to remind her all that info is available on the Internet. "Did you need something?"

"Sure do. I need a friend in this town. I've decided to stay here for a while, and I want some advice on where to look for a place."

I confess that I feel a little peeved at her. I can't help wondering if Melvin Barnes would still be alive if he hadn't run into Allie Saturday night. Oh, my heavens! Suicide or accident? That's what Wayne said, but what if Mrs. Barnes's thrown drink is just the tip of her anger iceburg? The principal's wife comes across as a hard, cold woman. She's dealing with hurt and humiliation, but could she have caused the hanging? That doesn't make sense. Melvin Barnes sent her home.

"Well," I say to Allie. "I'm at work right now. Why don't I think about it and let you know if I have any ideas about where you could rent something. What do you have in mind? An apartment, a house, or just a room."

"Renting will mean signing a lease, and I don't plan to stay that long. You don't happen to want a roommate for a few weeks, do you?"

"That doesn't matter. I rent, and it's in my lease that I live alone." Okay, so that's a lie. Well, at least half a lie. I do rent, but there's nothing in my lease about a roommate. Jane was even my roommate there for a short while years ago. The thing is, if, and I say *if* I did want anyone living with me, it would be Wayne. Another thing, I'd be a fool to move in someone who can switch from plain to seductress as easily as Alice does. I like her and I feel sorry about her sister and parents, but her actions Saturday night bother me.

"Okay, just thinking. How about lunch? Do you get a break?"

"Not at a specific time. I've got your cell number here on caller ID. If you'll be nearby, I'll call you when I know what time I'll be free."

"Don't you get the bodies ready? Are you working on Melvin now?"

"I do help prepare the decedents for their loved ones, but I'm not working on anyone right now."

"Will you call me when you can go to lunch?"

"I'll call."

"Promise?"

"Yes, I promise."

She disconnects first, and I'm left pondering how much the end of that call sounded like I was talking to a child, not a grown woman, and I do mean *grown* as evidenced by Saturday night.

My usual work at Middleton's making decedents look beautiful for their families and people who love them almost always gives me pleasure. I like the fact that everyone who works at Middleton's Mortuary is totally respectful toward the people we deal with—both the deceased and the survivors. When a death has been especially brutal, Otis or Odell help me with reconstruction, though I'm becoming more and more skilled in those situations. Knowing all that, I still feel hesitant about working on Melvin Barnes, but I go to our clothing room and select a navy blue suit, white shirt, and blue striped necktie. The thought crosses my mind that Melvin might look nice if we bury him in that powder blue tux he wore Saturday night, but I mentally scold myself for even thinking such a thing. It was probably rented.

The rest of the morning is quiet. No phone calls and no paperwork for me to do, so I read my book and wait for lunchtime. At noon, I go to the prep room and ask if it's okay for me to take my lunch hour now. I consciously avoid looking at Melvin Barnes's body lying on the prep table.

"Sure," Odell answers me. "How about bring us back some sandwiches?"

"Any particular kind?" I ask, knowing Odell will want barbecue. Doesn't matter if it's pepper/vinegar, red sauce, or mustard sauce.

Sure enough, he says, "Barbecue, and I'm starving, so make it two." He pauses before adding, "Or three."

"Two sandwiches will be plenty for you," Otis reprimands Odell. "One of these days you're gonna weigh six hundred pounds. Don't expect me to bring food to you when you can't get out of bed. I won't be your enabler on that television show where the doctor operates on fat people."

"Well, Doofus, if I ever get that big, all of this

will belong to you." He waves his arm around the room.

"What do you want, Otis?" I ask, trying to put an end to their brotherly bickering.

"Grilled chicken with lettuce and tomato on wheat."

"Okay," I tell them. "I'll go to Another Barbecue."

"Don't take more than an hour," Odell says as I leave. "I'm starving."

"You're *always* starving," Otis tells him.

ALLIE MUST HAVE BEEN somewhere near Another Barbecue when we spoke because she's already seated when I come in.

The naming of Another Barbecue is a well-known story around St. Mary. When Bubba Andrews decided to open a small restaurant in St. Mary, he didn't want to call it Bubba's Barbecue because there was already one of those owned by another guy called Bubba in a nearby town. After much discussion and an actual contest run by a local DJ, Bubba Andrews named his place Another Barbecue though the winning suggestion had been Just Another Barbecue.

"Hi, Allie," I say, "you changed your hair color." It's clearly several shades lighter—a strawberry blond.

"What else does a woman do when she's alone at a B & B and gets bored? I did it myself with a drugstore kit." She touches a curl that's peeking from behind her ear. "I wanted it to be darker to go with that red dress Saturday night, so I rinsed in temporary color. It didn't all come out, so I stripped it down to this. Do you like it?"

"Sure do," I answer. I almost tell her that I'll do her color for her next time, but there's something about Allie that makes me hesitate to offer to spend a lot of time with her. Some women automatically pull away from others who are flashier or better looking. Surely I'm not that shallow. Then again, Allie definitely outshined me Saturday night, but I wouldn't trade my life for hers for a million dollars.

Without waiting for a response, Allie adds, "This is a cute place with all the pink pig pictures on the walls. So many new places in town since I left."

"Well, over twenty-five years is a long time. Bubba Andrews, who owns this place, was probably in kindergarten when you went off to college."

"Have you eaten here before?" she asks.

"Lots of times."

"The menu isn't very big."

"It's strictly barbecue. Lots of barbecue buffets in the South have fried chicken, potato salad, collards, and other things, but Bubba doesn't offer a buffet and his menu is limited. Here it's barbecued pork or chicken with your choice of sauce. The only sides are rice and hash, coleslaw, and rolls."

"What are you having?"

"The barbecue is good, but I always have a hash and rice plate with coleslaw and a roll."

"I think I'll have the same thing. I like hash, and haven't had it in years. Not many places out of the Southeast have it."

I'd heard that before, but having lived in South Carolina my entire life, I always expect a barbecue place to serve rice and hash. We order, and I add two barbecue sandwiches with both mustard and red sauce on the side, a bare barbecue chicken sandwich with lettuce and tomato, and two orders of coleslaw to go for Otis and Odell.

"What's 'bare' barbecue chicken?" Allie asks.

"Chicken that's been slow smoked but has no sauce."

While we wait for food, Allie mentions becoming my roommate again. I assure her that I can't have one.

"What's wrong with the B & B if you're only going to stay a month or so?" I ask.

"I want more privacy," Allie replies. "There's only one bathroom for each two bedrooms. There was some fuss last night about how long I was in there when I colored my hair."

Downing about half of my Diet Coke, I suggest, "How about a regular motel room? The Sleep Easy Inn is convenient, and you'd have your own facilities as well as a continental breakfast each morning."

"I may look into that," she says, and then she brings up the real reason for this meeting.

"When I spoke with the sheriff yesterday, I asked him about my sister Josie's case. I wanted him to reopen it. He said that it's not closed. Called it a cold case, but still open. Then I asked if I could read the file. He said a flat no. Since you and he are close, I wonder if he'd be willing to let you see it."

There it is. Why Allie wants me to be her "friend."

As the server puts our plates in front of us, I tell Allie, "There's no way. Wayne is very by-the-book. He'd never let me read the file on an open case."

"Will you try to talk him into assigning a detective to take another look at Josie's death?"

"I'll do better than that. I'll try to convince him to do it himself."

"Oh, would you? That would be great."

As we eat, I try to learn more about Alice Lara Patterson. "Allie," I say, "I'm curious about the past twenty-seven years in your life. Are you married? Do you have children?"

"Never married and no kids. I've really been clinically depressed most of my life since I left here."

"What kind of work do you do? How can you just take a month or so off to stay here in St. Mary and look into what happened?"

"I taught."

"I did, too. A kindergarten teacher until my divorce. Then I came back here and worked at a beauty parlor until I got my job at Middleton's."

"I don't understand how you can stand working in a funeral home. Why do you do it?"

"Most of the time, I enjoy creating a beautiful memory for the people who have lost a loved one. Besides, I was tired of five-year-olds who wouldn't sit still or be quiet for their naps. At Middleton's, everyone I work on lies motionless and no one has to get up and go tee tee every five minutes."

The look on Allie's face shows me I've made a big mistake telling her that. Her expression is shock and revulsion. I should remember that, like cop humor, mortuary humor is only amusing to those who work in the field. Thank heaven I didn't tell her that the only times working as a cosmetician at a funeral home upsets me is when I have to work with deceased children. That would surely send her mind right to her little sister Josie's death.

"What about now?" I ask. "You're not teaching this school year?"

"No, I took early retirement in June. I actually considered cleaning up the family farm and moving out there, but I haven't even been to the property yet. I've paid the taxes each year, but I imagine after so many years just sitting there, the buildings are probably in bad shape."

Not wanting to speculate on how dilapidated a house and barns would be after almost thirty years of neglect, I ask, "What grade did you teach?"

"Secondary English, usually tenth grade. That's what I was talking to Melvin about at the reunion—the possibility of teaching or even subbing for St. Mary High School." She finished the last bite of her rice and hash. "Did Wayne tell you anything about how Melvin died?"

"No, he doesn't talk about cases with me." I'm not comfortable to say anything about the Google search John showed me.

She squirts some mustard barbecue sauce on her plate and dips her roll into it. That's a new one for me. "I heard he hanged himself," she says and then bites off the part of the roll that's dripping sauce.

"I think that might have been in the newspaper, but Wayne doesn't talk to me about it." I decide to change the subject before I forget my manners and question her about her shameless appearance and behavior at the reunion. "What about hobbies? What do you like to do?" I ask.

"I write. I've sold a few short stories, and I thought I might try a novel now that I've retired, but I'm not thinking I want to stay here the rest of my life even if living in the farm house would make my retirement check go further."

"Do you still own your family's property?"

"It's mine. I'll probably go out and take a look at it, but I'm not in a hurry to do that. When I decided to come to the reunion, I thought I'd check out the house and move in, maybe teach or sub here while I work on the book, but it's all too sad."

"I can understand that." I look at the clock on the wall—one with a pink pig painted on it. The pig's tail is the hour hand and it's rapidly approaching one o'clock.

"This was fun," I say, "but I have to get back to work."

Chapter Eight

I TELL ALLIE I'M GOING BACK TO WORK, but things don't turn out that way.

On return to Middleton's, I notice an old white Ford Econoline in front of me with a magnetic sign on the side that reads *Animal Rescue*. Maybe they've picked up Big Boy. I decide to stop them and ask. I blow the horn, but instead of stopping, the Econoline speeds up. When I attempt to pull around on the left, it veers off to the right and makes a screeching, skidding noise as it turns off the road onto what appears to be nothing more than a driveway. By the time I'm able to turn around and follow, it's gone.

I slow down and continue on my way, but only a few minutes later, Otis calls and tells me that Ty has been blowing up the funeral home phone wanting to know if I can come to the high school to help plan the haunted graveyard in the lot adjacent to the St. Mary High School football field parking lot.

"He also said he asked you to lend him a casket and you refused," Otis adds.

"That's exactly right," I answer, expecting him to commend me for that answer.

"Well, you did what you should have, but Odell and I talked about it, and we want to help the kids, too. Remember a while back when those thieves got into the warehouse and one of them slept in a casket?"

"Of course, I remember that."

"Well, that casket can't be sold and is still in the back of the warehouse. Odell and I loaded it in the old van. Come by here and switch your car for the van. We're giving the casket to the high school Fall Festival and we're willing to store it in the warehouse between Octobers."

Dalmation! I dang near wet my underpants. Why didn't I think of that?

"Did you tell Tyrone all that?" I ask in astonishment.

"No, you can tell him, but there's one condition. This is an anonymous donation. No one is to know where it came from."

STRANGE HOW A PERSON can see something for years and simply not notice it. Just beyond the football field, behind the parking lot, is an empty lot I've never paid attention to before. A sagging ruin of a picket fence well on its way to being reclaimed by nature encloses the field. That's a polite way to say it's rotting and falling down. I park and walk over to where Mr. Douglas stands in the midst of several teenagers.

I recognize some of the kids from last Saturday. Today, they're wearing boots instead of tennis shoes as they tromp through the brown tangle of overgrown undergrowth, swinging scythes. Zack, the one who accused Tyrone of hurting me so he could drive my car must be trying out a costume for the Fall Festival. He's tall and lean with a sharp, aquiline nose and a wide, thin-lipped mouth. His features are perfect to go with his costume which includes a black frock coat over a dark velvet shirt and black dress pants. Long, tapering fingers end with black-polished nails, and his ponytail is as dark as the nail polish.

He, Ty, and two more classmates huddle around Mr. Douglas, who is writing on a clipboard. Other kids are cutting and painting materials spread out on the ground, making crosses and tombstones out of cardboard and Styrofoam. Three girls twist wires clustering tissue flowers to create fake casket sprays.

"Hello, everyone," I say as I approach them.

"How are you, Ms. Parrish?" Mr. Douglas asks. "I'm still sorry you were hurt. I feel like it's my fault."

"I'll be fine." I gesture toward the field. "I assume this is going to be the cemetery."

"Yes, we're planning costumes for the students to wear. Of course, Zack here won't need a costume. He can wear his everyday clothes." Mr. Douglas grins and motions toward the student in black. He taps his ballpoint pen on the clipboard. "This may turn out to be better than the haunted house would have." He looks at the kids around him. "What do you guys think?"

Amid multiple responses of, "Yes," "Much better," and, "Best ever," Ty asks me, "Why are you driving Middleton's van? Is the Vette broken down?"

"Oh, no," I answer, "I've brought a surprise for the TEAM class."

As though they'd been given a command to move to the van, the kids all rush over. Mr. Douglas and I follow them. I open the back of the vehicle and motion toward the gray steel casket.

"Are you letting us use this?" Ty asks in disbelief.

"Not really me. Someone is donating it to the school."

The expression on Mr. Douglas's face is priceless, a combination of pleasant surprise and hesitation or even fear.

"What's the matter?" one of the girls asks the teacher.

"I'm wondering where we'll keep it after the

festival," Mr. Douglas answers. "I can guarantee you my wife won't let me put it in our garage."

"I'll store it," Zack says. He laughs. "I might even sleep in it."

"The Middletons will store it for you," I guarantee them. "There is a condition though. They don't want to be recognized in any way." I don't bother to explain that my bosses take death and funerals solemnly and don't want their establishment to be associated with frivolity.

"We can do that," Mr. Douglas assures me and then motions for the kids to gather closer around him. "We were working on what we need to set this up to look like a graveyard, who'll be in charge of each station, and what costumes they'll wear."

A pretty teenager says, "We're so happy it's working out. Ty suggested making it a cemetery, and Mr. Douglas got permission for us to use this space. They were throwing away a bunch of white tissue flowers from the gym. We saved them and we'll make more out of other colors. My mom's going to show us how to make flowers out of crepe paper like these."

Immediately my mind goes to the crepe paper poppies around the skull at the Halsey house, but I hold my tongue.

"And we're digging a fresh grave for someone to jump out of," says a student holding a shovel.

"We can put that casket in the hole," another one suggests and points toward the open back of the van.

"Let's stick with our plan to build a plywood casket for the grave. We'll use the real one somewhere more visible, where it will be seen better," suggests Mr. Douglas. "Do you have any ideas, Ms. Parrish?"

"Ty and I talked about zombies. On the way over, it occurred to me that the zombies could seem to appear out of smoke if you rent a fog machine like rock bands use."

"Good idea." Mr. Douglas makes a note.

"We'll still dig a grave and have someone pop out of it," Zack says.

"Or . . ." a girl announces dramatically. "We could dig a hole, cover it with something that looks like turf and have a hand reach through the covering and grab people's ankles as they walk by."

"You could put the real casket on a bier and do a fake funeral scene. Then have the 'corpse' sit up," I suggest.

The students' confused expressions puzzle me until Ty asks, "Beer? What do you mean? We'd put the casket on top of cases or on a keg? I don't think the school will let us do that."

I have to laugh though I hope it doesn't embarrass him. "Not beer—b-e-e-r. I'm saying bier—b-i-e-r. It's the stand that a casket sits on during services."

"Oh, can you get us one of those?" another student asks.

"Best be grateful for the donation of the casket and not ask for anything else. My bosses won't want anything used that they will ever need to use again for a real funeral, but a bier is only a stand." I motion toward the stack of plywood. "You can build one from some of that."

The kids stop talking and stare at me. I can tell they're waiting for another idea, but I'm experiencing brain flatulence. Then, as though I have good sense, I volunteer.

"I can stay awhile and help make the markers if you'd like."

"Sure," Mr. Douglas tells me, then turns toward the kids. "Everybody, let's get that coffin out of the van."

They unload the casket. Mr. Douglas throws a tarp over it so that it won't be visible to anyone who passes by. "Now get back to work," he says. "We have a lot to do before Saturday." He motions toward a young man holding a shovel. "Aeden, you and Tyrone can get busy digging that hole. It needs to be what, Ms. Parrish? About six feet long by three feet wide?"

"That should do it, but it won't have to be six feet deep if you're going to do the bit with someone reaching out and grabbing people. Maybe two and a half feet deep at the most. The person inside can lie down."

The next hour passes quickly as I help Vanessa and Taylor spray paint Styrofoam crosses and write on cardboard markers. Vanessa holds one up for me to read:

Here lies Will
Who caught a chill
That made him ill
Now here lies Will

I giggle as though I'm no older than my co-workers.

Eeeeeeeeeeeee euuuuuuh! The shriek cuts across the field like a knife through butter on a hot South Carolina day. I jump up as quickly as Vanessa and Taylor, and we rush toward the sound. The screamer is Tyrone, but I don't see him. When we reach the pseudo-grave, I see why. Two strong young men can dig quickly and deeply. Ty is at the bottom of a hole much deeper than I would expect so soon. Aeden and Zack are on their knees, leaning out, reaching for Ty, easily within reach. Tyrone ignores the grasping hand and yells again.

After the screech, I distinguish words.

"Another one, another one!"

I bend over just in time to see Tyrone throw something toward me. I don't mistake this one for a white pumpkin. It's dirty—discolored to an earthtone that matches the dead weeds we stand in.

It bounces off my chest and falls to the ground, leaving smudges of dirt on my black dress.

"What's that?" Aeden asks.

"It's another skull, or at least part of one," Ty says and reaches for Aeden's still outreached hand.

I pick up a stick from the ground, carefully insert it into an eyehole, and lift the remnants of the top of a head. The lower jaw is missing. A small piece near where an ear would be breaks off and falls to my feet.

"Look at that," Aeden says as he hauls Ty up to ground level. "Ms. Parrish did that just like a cop."

"Her boyfriend is the sheriff," Ty comments as if that's why I know better than to touch the skull. Actually, what difference would it make? Surely there are no fingerprints on this dirty piece of bone. Tyrone barely reaches the surface when he pulls his cell phone from his pocket and hits speed dial.

"Rizzie? Ty here. Is Mr. Everett there?"

A pause as he listens.

"We're behind the football field at the school, and we just found another skull, only this one looks even more real and a lot older. Will you ask him if he'll come over here?"

Another moment of silence, and then Ty disconnects and looks at us. "My sister's friend is headed this way. He's an archaeologist and will know if that's real or not." He gestures toward me, but I know he's referring to the skull, not to my inflated chest.

"Call the sheriff's department, too," I tell him.

Mr. Douglas herds all the kids into a cluster. I know "herds" is a strange word to use here, but growing up on a farm, I saw animals herded to the barn when storms were expected. I was always amazed when some would dally and my dad or one of my brothers would be sure they joined the group again. The kids keep detouring past the hole before heading to Mr. Douglas. They peer down inside it, but there's nothing to see since Ty climbed out.

Surprised when Wayne drives up because I really expect a deputy instead of the sheriff, I walk toward his cruiser still carrying the skull on the stick. That thought makes me laugh. I'm a big fan of Jeff Dunham and really like Jose, the Jalapeno on a Stick. I don't think he's politically correct, but I'm not either.

Wayne steps out holding a large sack. When he reaches me, he takes the stick in hand and slides the skull into the bag. He opens his mouth to speak, but before a word is out, Bob Everett pulls up in a fairly new forest green Jeep and dashes over to us. Well, he dashes as much as even a fit old man can.

"Let me see that," Bob demands, reaching for the skull.

"Who are you?" Wayne asks.

"I'm Robert Everett, an archaeologist doing research in this area. I believe you're holding a valuable piece of history there. Eight tribes of

Native Americans have members still living in South Carolina, but several tribes are extinct. You may have proof of one of those tribes or even another one right there."

"Or I may have evidence of a crime," Wayne says, pointedly moving the evidence bag away from Bob.

"I'd really like to take a closer look at the skull," Bob says.

"Or maybe you'd really like to get this piece of evidence out of my custody and into your own hands." Wayne's eyes narrow. "You say you're an anthropologist. Can you prove that?"

"Of course I have documentation of both of my professional affiliations, but I'm an archaeologist also. The fields overlap at times." Bob fumbles into the pocket of his shorts and comes up empty-handed before adding, "I'm afraid I don't have my wallet with me."

"So you drove that Jeep over here without your driver's license?" The sheriff's accusing tone is hard to miss.

"This is silly," I say. "Bob, this is Wayne Harmon, Sheriff of Jade County. Wayne, meet Robert Everett. He's here doing research on the coastal area."

"Says who?" Wayne asks. "I'd like some proof."

"Ask me an anthropological or archaeological question," Bob suggests.

"Name the Native American tribes living in

FRAN RIZER

South Carolina." Wayne grins as though he's said something brilliant.

"The Catawba, Pee Dee, Chicora, Edisto, Santee, Yamassee, and Chicora-Waccamaw are still represented in this state as well as many descendants of the Cherokee. My work is with discovering other tribes that lived here and are now extinct. I assure you that I can determine if that skull is from an old burial ground or is more recent."

"Well, you may get your chance, but first, Mr. Douglas, you need to get these young folks out of this area. I'm going to have deputies seal the lot off with crime scene tape until we know what we're dealing with here. That skull could be evidence of a crime or . . . " He nods toward Bob. "If this is of historical significance, I'll need to notify the proper authorities. Especially if it's Native American. There are laws about removing things from ancient burial grounds."

His words are met with moans and calls of dismay from the teenagers.

"Cut that out," Mr. Douglas scolds. "Meet back on the steps of the school tomorrow morning at ten and we'll regroup."

"Wayne, you're ruining their plans," I say.

"Murder is more important than a class project," Wayne says.

"So is history," Bob adds.

"I agree," Wayne tells him.

"Can I go now?" I ask.

"Where are you headed?" Wayne asks.

"To take the van back to Middleton's, but on the way, I'm driving around looking for Big Boy."

"Want to get together for dinner? Unless we find the rest of an almost fresh skeleton here, I should be available around seven."

"Where?" I ask.

"Anywhere you say."

"Rizzie's."

"Okay, see you then." His tone is dismissive. He turns away and begins giving deputies directions to surround the students' haunted graveyard with yellow crime scene tape.

A PHONE CALL TO MIDDLETON'S gives me permission to drive the van the rest of the day and leave the Vette parked in my space at the funeral home. I ride and ride and ride, but no sign of Big Boy or the white Econoline.

By the time I reach the grill, I'm hoarse from screaming my dog's name out the window. Ty greets me at the door demanding, "Has the sheriff released the lot yet? This isn't fair for him to keep taking our space from us."

"It's not the sheriff's fault that you keep finding skulls," I snap back. I'm not angry with him. I'm furious that there's no sign of my dog. Wayne's telling me he thinks the dog was stolen disturbs me, and the thought of my Big Boy being victim of a hit-and-run takes my mind to Allie and her sister. I can't imagine the absolute horror of losing her sister that way, especially the part about medical reports indicating she bled out and death was slow and probably agonizing.

Rizzie calls Ty back to the kitchen, and I sit in a booth by myself. I'm thinking. My thoughts are on homicide, a murder unsolved after more than a quarter of a century. Who knows? Maybe the hit-and-run was a true accident. Maybe Allie's little sister rode out in front of whatever vehicle hit her and the driver couldn't stop in time. That's possible, but when the child was left bleeding out, that possible accident became a murder in my mind.

I love the food at Rizzie's Gastric Gullah Grill, but I wish I'd told Wayne to meet me somewhere else—somewhere more private. Sure enough, Robert Everett comes in only a few minutes later.

"Hi, mind if I join you?" he asks as he slides into the seat across from me.

I do object, but I don't tell him. He sits across from me. I hope he won't stay the whole time Wayne and I are here.

"I understand," Bob says, "that you and the sheriff are an item. I'd really like to examine those skulls, and I have the certification to prove I'm qualified. Do you think you could put in a word for me with him?"

Dalmation! Everybody wants to use me to get to Wayne just because we're dating. "Everybody" is an exaggeration, but Allie Patterson and Bob

Everett are too many for me.

"I'm sorry," I answer, "but I don't get involved in Wayne's work at all." I do try sometimes, but it never works anyway. He won't let me.

"I have some more information about Gullah root work," he says. "I don't want to talk about it in front of Rizzie though. I can't figure out exactly what's going on with that, but she's not comfortable talking about it. I . . ."

He stops mid-sentence and looks over his shoulder. Jane heads toward us, looking cute in her apron and white chef's hat. Her mobility cane swishes back and forth gently as she finds her way.

"Hi, Callie," she says.

"Hello yourself," I answer. "What's the specialty tonight?"

"One of your favorites—Italian meatball stew."

"That's what I'll have then, but hold the order until Wayne gets here. He's meeting me."

"Callie, I need you to do me a favor. I'm thinking about writing a recipe book, and . . ."

I lol—a great big belly laugh. "Jane, you and I both know there's no way you want a recipe from me." The truth is that the reason I eat so many Moon Pies is because my cooking is worse than bad. That's why I only try very simple dishes and still goof them up most of the time.

Jane smiles. "No, I don't want a recipe. I want a neat, computer-printed sign to put up in here and some handouts. Rizzie says it's okay."

"And what should the sign say?"

"Something like *Jane Baker is looking for ground meat recipes to serve here at Gastric Gullah Grill and publish in her first cookbook. Submitters of selected recipes will be given credit both on the menu and in the book. Submissions accepted only by email to 'The Extra Ingredient' by Jane Baker.*"

She pauses before adding, "And then give my email address."

"I'll make it for you," I answer her, thinking I'll do it at work. I have a PC and printer at home, but the mortuary's computer has more bells and whistles. I don't bother to ask why only email entries will be taken. I know Jane well enough to know that she's so independent she doesn't want anyone having to read to her. The computer at her apartment reads emails to her, and she's an efficient keyboarder.

"Callie," Jane's voice fills with enthusiasm. "You realize that I could be surrounded by signs and not know it, but have you posted reward posters about Big Boy?"

"I haven't seen any," Bob says.

Daddy used to quote Forrest Gump all the time. Forget about the chocolates. The line for me today is, "Stupid is as stupid does." The very first thing I should have done is plaster the area with signs about Big Boy.

I'm too embarrassed to acknowledge I didn't think of missing-dog signs, so I go back to her request. "I'll make your recipe notices right away."

"Both a sign and handouts?"

"A sign and some flyers."

I should have ordered my meatball stew and eaten without waiting for Wayne because as it turns out, I won't be eating for a long time. A call from Odell to pick up a removal snatches me away from Rizzie's. Guess I should have gone back by Middleton's and traded the van for my car after all.

Chapter Nine

I'VE BEEN HERE BEFORE. *Déjà vu.* Several years ago, my very first removal (Funeraleze for picking up a body from the place of death and taking it to the funeral home or to Charleston for an autopsy) was from this house. The call was for a man who drowned in his hot tub. It turned out that he was my pharmacist and he'd been poisoned. No chance of that here.

Same hot tub. Just like the first time, a corpse lies in the water, and as before, hair floats on top of the liquid. That time, it was white. This time, it's red hair—the color of Allie Patterson's before she colored it, but shorter, much shorter.

"They sent *you?*" Wayne asks when I walk over to the hot tub. I'm sure it's the same one as before.

"That sounds kind of insulting," I say.

"I just mean your job is to dress and cosmetize. I'd just as soon Otis and Odell not send you out to pick up bodies."

"I do removals when necessary, and since I'm driving the van, they called me. My car is back at the mortuary. Who is this?" I ask.

"Norman Clark."

"The fire chief?" I ask.

"Yes, and Amick is calling the death accidental. No question about it this time. Norman foolishly attached a bug zapper light to that tree branch above the tub. The zapper was too heavy and dropped into the water with its live wire."

Now I'm not making judgments here, but that doesn't sound like the man who was in charge of the town fire department was thinking at all when he did that. "I thought accidents like this were old wives' tales and made-up stories for murder mysteries, like when someone throws the radio or hair dryer into the bathtub while the music's playing or the dryer is blowing. Myth Busters even did a show about it."

"Made perfect sense to the cops who were here first and to the firemen. Coroner has come and gone already and declared the death. Cause is electrocution. Manner is accidental. Not even asking for an autopsy."

"I thought any death that isn't natural requires an autopsy."

"That's true, but it's the coroner's call and he's ticked off that some of us are disagreeing with his

FRAN RIZER

decision to call Melvin's death a suicide. We believe it's accidental, and personally, I think too many people are just wanting to gossip about it. A cover-up may not be legal, but sometimes, it's the kindest thing to do."

"A cover-up?" I'm eager to engage Wayne in a discussion about this.

He cuts me a look that shouts he's not going to discuss it and says, "Don't ask."

I back up a few steps from the hot tub and question, "How am I supposed to get him out of the water to transport him? Is there still electricity in it?"

"Do you see the water moving?"

I lean over and look, being careful not to get too close. Even that's too near for me. The chemical smell of chlorine is strong.

"No," I answer, not understanding how that answers my question.

"If there were still any power, the water would be moving from the jets. When the zapper fell into the tub, it tripped the main breaker, stopping all power to the tub."

I point to the yard lights. "Then how are those lights burning?"

"Electrician came and restored power except to the hot tub and the zapper. I think one of the firemen could have done that, but they're all too upset."

I don't ask anything, just give him a questioning look.

"The firemen are upset because Norman is, or I should say *was,* the fire chief," one of the deputies says.

"I was here another time a few years back when the pharmacist died," I say and motion toward a driveway beside the house. "I backed the van through there. Can I do that again?"

"It's all right with me," Wayne says.

"Who reported the death?" I ask as I unload the church truck (Funeraleze for a rolling gurney used to move bodies). The body bags are waterproof, but Mr. Clark is sopping wet, so I'll want to use a disaster pouch which is thicker and heavier-duty. I get everything I need out of the van and since no one has answered my question, I ask it again. "Who reported the death?"

"UPS man. He's delivered to Clark before when he was in the tub. Brought a box from Amazon and came around back when he saw the car in the driveway but got no answer at the front door."

For the first time, I look around at the crowded backyard. Sure enough, in addition to deputies, EMTs, and firemen, a young man in a khaki uniform is standing over by the back door of the house. He looks like a deer caught in the headlights. His eyes dart all over the yard as though looking for an escape. I can't help it. I wonder if he had anything to do with the fireman's death. Then I realize that most folks would probably react that way to finding someone dead. It's just that I've done it so often that I don't react as strongly as might be expected. I catch the man's eye and then walk over to him.

"Guess you're who found the body?" I ask.

"That would be me. My name's Ben, and I think you and I met when Middleton's Mortuary handled my Mee Maw's funeral." He swallows hard and asks, "Do you know when I can get out of here?"

"I thought you looked familiar. You can leave as soon as the lead investigator or sheriff says it's okay."

"I just want to leave. I've got more deliveries, but I'm going to call in sick when I go. I've delivered lots of packages here, and when Mr. Clark is at home and not at the fire department, I usually walk around back. Mr. Clark was always bragging about how much the hot tub helped his arthritis. I remember asking him wouldn't it be too cold to be outside like that before long, and he said it was never too cold because the water warmed him when he got in."

Wayne dismisses the delivery man before he lets me remove Mr. Clark. By the time we have the Speedo-wearing fire chief out of the water and double-bagged, I'm drenched. I take him to Middleton's and switch the van for my Vette as soon as Mr. Clark is unloaded.

It's too late to go to Rizzie's for my meatball stew, so I go through the all night drive-through McDonald's for a Quarter Pounder with Cheese, still my favorite from their menu. On the chance that Wayne didn't have the opportunity to eat either, I pick up a fish fillet sandwich for him. He tries to avoid red meat.

THE WAY TO A MAN'S HEART might be through his stomach, but the way to get Wayne Harmon to talk isn't by feeding him fish sandwiches when he shows up after midnight. The best thing with Wayne is to snuggle up to him after the loving but before he's snoring. I've read that a lot of men don't like cuddling, but the sheriff loves it.

"Wayne?" I say softly.

"Yes."

"I know you can't talk about cases, and I'm not going to pester you about Josie Patterson's or Melvin Barnes's deaths, but there's one thing that really bothers me."

"What's that? I'll answer one, and only one, question."

Shih tzu! I don't say it out loud because even though that's a breed of dog and it's technically kindergarten cussing, Wayne doesn't like for me to say that. He's okay if I blurt out *Dalmation* or *A Hundred and One Dalmations,* which is the special profanity I developed when I taught five-year-olds, though I didn't say even those things around my students. Wayne is kind of like my dad who thinks I shouldn't say anything un-lady-like around *anybody.* I haven't figured out if that's because I'm his girlfriend or because he's known me my whole life.

"Just one?" I ask, intentionally putting on a little-girl voice—not quite a Miss Magnolia Mouth, but definitely playing the innocent.

"Only one."

There are so many things I want to know. Like were there any leads concerning who ran over Josie Patterson. Like why were the coroner and the sheriff disagreeing on the manner of Melvin Barnes' death. Only one question. What to ask? What to ask?

"Sweetie, you'd better ask your question soon. I'm sleepy."

"I really need more than one question."

"One, and if you take too long, your answer will be the sound of me snoring."

"The newspaper said the principal's body was found in his office and he died of asphyxiation, but I want to know what he hanged himself with. I read some more about what John hinted at, but did Melvin have materials in his office to do that? Do you think it was a regular habit of his?"

"Okay," Wayne says with a sigh of resignation, "Melvin died due to asphyxiation as a result of hanging himself with a nylon jump rope."

"A jump rope? He kept a jump rope in his office?"

"A box of field day supplies was moved from the gym into Melvin's office when they cleaned up to decorate for the reunion. The big, fat ropes for the tug-of-war were in the box along with jump ropes. Melvin hanged himself with a jump rope— a Double Dutch rope that was cut to desired length."

"Then why do you think it's accidental?"

"I don't think he meant to die. I believe he was going for a happier happy ending." He kisses my cheek. "Now, go to sleep and stop worrying about it. Either way, it's a shame for him to leave this earth however it happened. He achieved a lot for the school and the community, and now, no matter how Amick tries to cover it up, Barnes will be remembered for his death instead of his life."

I open my mouth to ask more, but Wayne stops me with butterfly kisses.

Tuesday, October 27

Chapter Ten

"WHAT'S ON YOUR AGENDA for today?" Wayne asks as he buttons up his shirt.

"I have to go in to work this morning and dress Melvin Barnes. Then we'll probably be dealing with the fire chief. This afternoon, I'm working Melvin Barnes's funeral."

"What's up with that? I was surprised when the news article said it will just be graveside. There wasn't even an obituary printed." He ties his necktie.

"Mrs. Barnes is embarrassed and humiliated. All she's having is a prayer and then she's taking the kids and leaving town." I snuggle down deeper under the covers, not ready to get up as early as Wayne does. I'll just lie here for a while before I start my day and enjoy the cup of coffee Wayne will bring to my bedside before he leaves.

"The assistant principal told me she asked him not to have any formal recognition for Melvin at the school," Wayne says as he straps on his holster. "She's opposed to anything, but I think to totally ignore his death will just add to the rumors." He leans across the bed and kisses me. "I'll try to finish up in time for dinner together tonight."

"Sounds good," I answer before adding, "please let me know if you find out anything about the missing dogs."

"Of course."

I FEEL NO GUILT that I don't get up and cook breakfast for Wayne when he spends the night here. He's a biscuit man, used to driving through Bojangles' or Hardee's on his way to work. I frequently eat a Moon Pie for breakfast or, when I've shopped, a bowl of Cinnamon Toast cereal.

Getting up without having Big Boy lying by the bed waiting for a morning head-rub before running to the back door to go out seems ominous as well as strange. The apartment feels empty without him.

In the kitchen, I refill my coffee cup and reach for a Moon Pie, but I change my mind and put it back in the cabinet. Today's going to be difficult under any circumstances. I remember the burns on the fire chief's body. He won't be easy to transform into a beautiful memory picture.

Mr. Barnes won't be easy either. The shirt collar will need to be adjusted high enough to cover bruises and abrasions around his neck. Yes, I know he's closed-casket and no one will see him except Middleton's employees, but I always try to create the best image possible. I wonder, too, how much his children know about his death and if they're as cavalier about his funeral as their mother. I recall from somewhere that the boy is ten years old and the girl is twelve.

After my hot shower, I pull my currently mahogany-brown hair into a loose updo at the back of my neck and put on one of my many simple black dresses that Otis and Odell insist I wear to work along with stockings and black leather low heels. I know that panty hose are out of fashion, but Otis would stroke out if I showed up at work bare-legged. A touch of lipstick and mascara, and I'm on my way.

There's no sound from Jane's apartment next door, and I note that Frankie's truck isn't parked in the drive today.

Since I left a few minutes early, I drive through the neighborhood looking out the window and calling for Big Boy, but there's no response. More and more, I fear Wayne is right that my dog was stolen.

Right before I turn into the drive at Middleton's, I notice a white Econoline behind me. It must not be the one I saw before because there is no sign on it.

"Good morning, Callie," greets me as I enter the back door.

"Morning, Odell," I reply, "what's first today?"

"I've already moved Mr. Barnes to your workroom. Let me know when he's ready and I'll help you casket him."

I put my prep clothing over my dress, making me look like a haz-mat worker. I used to wear only an all-over apron and mask while I worked, but times have changed.

Okay, so I'm human and sometimes curious. I lift the sheet covering Melvin Barnes and look at him lying there wearing only the new white boxer shorts that the Middletons always put on males before bringing them to me. The wounds are standard for an autopsy, but he also has deep indentations around his neck. I unseal and lift an eyelid to examine the tiny petechial spots of red that indicate choking. I can't help but feel sorry for his children. When they're older and understand how he died, the thought of death by strangulation will be painful for them.

I took as much care selecting clothing for Mr. Barnes as though he will be seen during a visitation. Since he chose blue for his "prom suit," I have already selected a white dress shirt, deep navy-toned suit, and a blue and white Jerry Garcia necktie. I'm not a big Grateful Dead fan, but I do love those ties.

When I buzz for Odell, he responds immediately with a middle-priced wooden casket.

There are funeral directors who would gouge the survivors for the most expensive coffin if possible. That's not Otis and Odell's way, and that's part of why I like working for them. After Mr. Barnes is casketed, we wheel the bier into the smallest slumber room which is seldom used.

Odell locks the door. "Why this room?" I ask. "Do you think we will be full by this afternoon?"

"No, Mr. Clark goes into A. We could put Mr. Barnes in B, but his wife specified that he is not to receive any visitors at all. She's furious that a reporter found out about the graveside services from one of our diggers. It's in the newspaper."

I have no answer for that. Part of me understands her anger, but some of me thinks maybe Melvin Barnes has paid the price for his indiscretion. Can't death be the final cost?

Back in my workroom, Otis brings in the fire chief. When I remove the sheet covering him I see that the burns are worse than I remembered and that skin is sloughing off like what we in the business call slippage when a person goes undiscovered for several days after death.

"Have plans been set for Mr. Clark?" I ask.

"Not yet. He's a bachelor, and his only survivor is a sister in Fayetteville, North Carolina. She's scheduled planning for this afternoon at five. I'll want you here for that."

"Should I go ahead and cosmetize or wait until after I see her?"

"She authorized preparation and she may

want to see him tonight. Do as much as you can, and I'll assist with any touch-up work when you finish."

Into work attire again, I begin covering up as much of the damage as I can. There are cases when cosmeticians have to restructure parts of bodies. This was more a rebuilding of the skin with occasional muscle involvement. I do the best I can and then buzz for Odell again. Otis comes instead.

I point to spots where my skill wasn't sufficient to create a normal look.

"That's okay, Callie. I'll work on those places." He pauses. "Did you think to order a floral casket spray for Mr. Barnes?"

I feel blood rush to my face. "No, I didn't." There's no need to try to explain. Otis knows that frequently the family takes care of that, but he also knows I should have checked on it.

Back at my desk, I call the florist and request the quickest arrangement possible. "Do you want to specify the kinds of flowers?" the clerk asks.

"No, anything suitable for a man—maybe blue." Then I realize that the spray doesn't need to coordinate with his suit. The casket will be closed. It's wooden, and it's better to match to the season. "Autumn colors," I say, "all kinds of golds and bronzes—fall flowers and leaves-- whatever you have on hand."

"I'll have it there in an hour," she assures me.

I barely disconnect the phone before Otis

comes in. "Unless you absolutely have to leave for lunch, I'd like you to stay through today."

"That's fine. I'll order something."

"I've already taken care of that. Domino's is delivering. Listen for them at the back door."

Like I don't know that anytime we order food, it comes to the back door. Pizza coming through the front door of a funeral home would be tacky, and that's one thing Middleton's never wants to be.

TWO AWNINGS SHELTER CHAIRS lined up neatly in front of Mr. Barnes's gravesite. Apparently Otis or Odell decided to prepare for some uninvited guests to show up after the plans were printed in the newspaper. Mr. Barnes's casket, topped by a large, beautiful arrangement of yellow spider mums and assorted smaller bronze blossoms with tiny orange accents, is already in place over the opening. I park and sit in the car, aware that my primary responsibility is to troubleshoot any unexpected drama during this brief service.

More and more cars park on the winding roads throughout Taylor's. I recognize some of the people who get out and walk toward Mr. Barnes's grave—Mr. Douglas, other teachers, town officials, Sam Blevins, Wayne, and lots more. So far no sign of Mrs. Barnes and her children. The chairs are soon filled except for the front row which is marked "Reserved." More people stand behind and beside the site.

I don't see a clergyman or perhaps I should say I don't see anyone wearing a collar or recognize a preacher from one of the other churches like Baptist whose pastors don't wear robes and collars.

For most services, even large ones, Otis, Odell, or I stay at the funeral home. I see Otis and Odell both standing near the casket. Since I'm here, too, they must have one of the part-timers tending the mortuary.

At last, a white BMW pulls up and stops in the middle of the roadway. Mrs. Barnes herself is driving. Otis opens the driver's door and Mrs. Barnes steps out wearing a beige dress with a black hat. It's obvious to me that she added the black veil herself because it's far thicker than any funeral veil I've ever seen. When Otis opens the back door, the young boy and girl who slide out are wearing what we here in the South call Sunday School clothes, but the girl has on a black hat like her mother's. Otis escorts the three of them to the front row, and then Odell steps forward.

I expect him to introduce whoever is officiating at the service. Instead, he says, "Dearly beloved, we are gathered here today to say farewell to Melvin Barnes." That's when I realize that Mrs. Barnes has turned Odell loose to "preach" the funeral. That might be a huge mistake as I can tell by his beginning the service as though it's a wedding. Thankfully, Odell keeps it short and simple with a brief Bible reading and the "ashes to ashes" quote. He ends with a prayer that's mighty close to my old bedtime "Now I lay me down to sleep."

When everyone realizes that this is it and there will be no homily or eulogy, they begin moving toward Mrs. Barnes and the children. She rushes the boy and girl back to the BMW, guns the motor, and leaves in a cloud of dust. She's barely gone before an Enterprise rental car pulls up to the angel statue marker at Josie Patterson's grave.

I breathe a prayer myself: *Thank you, God, that Allie didn't arrive before Mrs. Barnes left.*

Wayne comes over to me. "Well, that was strange," he says. "Otis told me that the Barnes family's pastor refused to do the service because Amick called the death a suicide, so he or Odell would have to speak."

"Different strokes for different folks," I say as if that might be appropriate, though the minute the words leave my mouth, I know they shouldn't have.

"How late are you working?" he asks.

"Planning for Mr. Clark with his sister at five. I should be out by six o'clock."

"Let's do dinner somewhere other than Rizzie's tonight. I'd just as soon not have to defend taping off the field to Tyrone or not calling in that Mr.

Everett to examine the skull. Actually, I'm planning to send it to the University of South Carolina in Columbia."

"Suits me. How about seven at Hudson's?"

"Sounds good. They have great salmon with a lime-dill sauce." He grins because while I love crab and other seafood, salmon is not one of my favorites. "But you can have steak if you prefer."

Mention of salmon makes me think of Daddy and Miss Ellen off fishing in Alaska. I miss my dad not being home when I want to talk to him.

SINCE I SKIPPED THE PIZZA before we went to Taylor's, I pop a slice into the microwave when I arrive back at the funeral home. A quick call on my cell phone to St. Mary Animal Rescue confirms that they still haven't picked up any Great Danes. I carry my pizza and a Diet Coke to my office and break my own rule not to eat while on the computer.

I soon have a poster designed for my missing dog. It gives his description and the number to reach me at Middleton's. I Google a photo of a Great Dane that looks a lot like Big Boy with similar black spots on his white coat and add it before printing off fifty of them. Otis and Odell won't mind because they've told me before to feel free to make copies at work.

The sign for Jane takes more thought. At last, I come up with a flyer describing her plans and a request for recipes using ground meat.

Although I feel comfortable printing my Big Boy signs at Middleton's since Otis and Odell have let me do similar things in the past, I email the cookbook flyer to Rizzie to print copies and enlarge one for a sign. The cookbook will benefit the grill, and I don't think Rizzie will mind doing that for Jane.

By the time I finish with those tasks, it's almost five o'clock. An instrumental version of the hymn "The Old Rugged Cross" announces that someone has entered the front door. I meet Otis in the hall as he welcomes an older lady with gray hair. She's a big woman, not fat, just tall and big-boned, wearing a pantsuit that is exactly the same shade as her hair and eyes and, I swear, the leather briefcase she carries is the same color.

I immediately think of two ghosts that Otis told me about. One of the best-known South Carolina apparitions is the Gray Man of Pawleys Island. He appears before severe storms as a warning, and it's said that those who see him will always survive the weather. Less known is the Gray Lady of Camden. That tale involves a Frenchman who tried to thwart his daughter's romance by putting her in a convent. She died there. Maybe because of a broken heart. I don't know. Anyway, her brothers came to America and settled near Camden in Kershaw County. Their family began seeing an apparition of a woman wearing the gray habit of nuns in France.

She was seen often until the inn founded by her siblings was destroyed in 1963. I've never seen either of these specters. I don't even know for a fact that I believe in ghosts, but the phrase "Gray Lady" pops to my mind when I see this woman.

"I'm Eva Clark, Norman Clark's sister," Gray Lady says and extends her hand.

Otis responds with, "We're so sorry for your loss, Ms. Clark. I'm Otis Middleton, and this is Callie Parrish. Let's step into the consultation room and discuss arrangements for Mr. Clark."

"I know exactly what I want, and I've brought a suit I want him to be wearing when I see him."

When we're seated in a planning room, Otis places his clipboard of forms on the table in front of us. I ask Ms. Clark, "Would you like something to drink? Perhaps coffee or a soda?"

"No, I just want to get this done." She points at Otis's papers. "You won't need all those. I've written my own obituary for Norman, and I know exactly what I want done with his body."

Otis smiles, but I can see that it's forced. "I'm required to enter the information on the forms and have you sign them, but we can speed things up as much as possible. May I see the obituary?"

Ms. Clark opens her case and pulls out several papers. Handing them to Otis, she says, "This is what I've already written, along with Norman's biographical data and a copy of his life insurance policy. I have clothing for him in my car. I want the obituary run in the newspapers and on the

Internet, and I want to see Norman, but nobody else is to view him."

As Otis shuffles through the papers she hands him, he asks, "Do you have a cemetery plot?"

"No, and we won't need one. He's to be cremated." She smiles. "Norm was a fireman because he loved fire. Mama had a horrible time keeping him from playing with matches when he was little. He and the kid across the street set the garage on fire when he was five years old. I think he'd rather be cremated than put beneath the ground."

I listen quietly as Otis and Ms. Clark discuss the visitation. She wants it to be at the funeral home and to serve "light" refreshments, including catered sandwiches cut into quarters with the crusts cut off, petit fours, coffee, and punch.

"A nonalcoholic punch," she specifies.

Otis notes all this and then asks, "What about the memorial service? Will you be using our chapel?"

"Oh, no. I don't want a memorial service." She shakes her head. "I want to add chips at the reception though. Chips with French onion dip. That was Norm's favorite."

That table is going to look like a bridal shower from the fifties, I think, but I keep my mouth shut, of course. Ms. Clark removes an 8" x 10" from her briefcase and hands it to Otis.

"These are pictures of Norman through the years. I want one of those slide presentations on a big screen television, and the music with it should be bluegrass gospel recordings. One of them is 'Will the Circle Be Unbroken?' I've brought an MP3 player with the songs already on it." She hands the player to Otis, and says, "That about does it. When can we have the reception?"

"Visitations used to always be the day or evening before the funeral or memorial service, but a lot of people prefer to have it for an hour or so just before the service begins." When Ms. Clark doesn't comment, Otis adds, "Would you prefer to select the casket from our catalog or do you want to see them in our display room?"

"I don't want a funeral nor a memorial service. The visitation will suffice. If Norm is being cremated, I don't really need a casket, do I?"

"No, ma'am. It won't be necessary unless you want him at the visitation." Otis looks a little rattled. "Or, of course, the urn with his cremains can be there."

Ms. Clark stands. "When will I be able to see my brother?"

"You authorized preparation by telephone, so embalming, which isn't legally required for a cremation without viewing, has been completed." I know Otis is covering for the mortuary when she gets the bill showing charges for prep which turns out not to be necessary in this case. Ms. Clark ignores that comment.

"I'd hoped to see him today, but I want you to put his suit on him first."

Does she think we'd just lay him out naked? I wonder. When there's to be no formal viewing, the family may see the deceased privately even without prep. We clean the remains and if clothes aren't provided, the funeral home supplies a simple cotton garment similar to a hospital gown.

"Where's the suit?" Otis asks.

"Out in my car."

Otis turns toward me. "Callie, go with Ms. Clark for the clothing. You can dress Mr. Clark and bring him to the chapel. Buzz me when you're ready for us."

"Oh, I don't need her to go with me," Ms. Clark protests. "I'll be back in a jiffy."

While she's gone, Otis tells me, "Mr. Clark is still in your workroom. As soon as he's dressed, move him to the chapel and let me know he's there."

I could have guessed what color Norman Clark's suit would be before I unzip the garment bag in my workroom—gray. I've known people who are overly partial to certain colors before. My favorite color has been purple since I was a little girl, and I've known other girls who are all into pink, but—gray?

The suit is the same shade as Ms. Clark's outfit. The shirt is a paler gray, and instead of a necktie, she's enclosed a gray and white polka-dotted clip-on bow tie. He's wearing standard new white boxers that Otis and Odell always put on decedents before moving them to my workroom. No socks or shoes in the garment bag, which wouldn't matter if I were putting him into a casket, but I'm not. I get some from our supply closet.

I use the body lift to raise Mr. Clark enough to allow me to pull the pants up and catch a glimpse of a dark patch across his back just at waist-line. I'm familiar with postmortem lividity, which is darkening of the skin when the blood pools at the lowest point where a body lies after death. I've seen that many, many times, but Mr. Clark has a rather prominent behind, a "baseball butt." I lower him and lying on his back, the space at his waist where the deep crimson mark is doesn't touch the table. I thought I'd seen everything, but this is new to me. I buzz for Otis, but Odell responds.

"Take a look at this, Odell." I lift the body again and point to Mr. Clark's lower back. "Is that livor mortis?"

"No, I don't think so. Looks more like an injury just before death." He leans over and peers more closely. "Isn't Ms. Clark waiting to see him?"

"That's right."

"Let's get him dressed, and we'll have Otis take a look to see what he thinks after she leaves."

With Odell's help, I finish with Mr. Clark's clothing and touch up his makeup. We place him on a gurney and drape a white satin coverlet over his legs and feet.

After we place Mr. Clark in the chapel, Odell goes for Otis and Ms. Clark.

Anytime someone views their deceased loved one, we are on the lookout for them to become emotional and grab the decedent. Normally, when I'm in attendance and think this is coming, I try to guide them to simply touch the hand. We don't want makeup smudged or to cause other problems. In this case, we'd done so much to smooth out and disguise charred, loosened skin that I really don't want her to touch him anywhere.

Ms. Clark stands silently, looking hard at her brother. "He looks different, somehow," she finally says.

My heavens, he's dead and he was electrocuted, I think. *We did the best we could, and I always try to create a beautiful memory picture, but you have no idea how he looked before. If you hadn't authorized embalming before deciding on cremation, we wouldn't have even cosmetized him without your specifying you wanted it.*

Odell senses what I'm thinking and pats me on the shoulder with his Undertaking 101 comfort touch as though I'm the bereaved.

Ms. Clark leaves with an assurance, "I'll be here tomorrow at two to make sure everything's like I want it for the visitation at three."

"Yes, ma'am."

While Otis walks Ms. Clark to her car, Odell

and I return Mr. Clark to my workroom. We place him on his stomach, lower his pants, and lift his jacket and shirt. When Otis comes in, he examines the spot and announces, "I think this mark is evidence that he suffered an injury before the electrification in the water. Callie, as soon as you've finished talking to the caterer and florist, call the sheriff and see if he'll come by and take a look at this. The coroner bypassed an autopsy, and to me, this injury wouldn't have been fatal. It probably won't change Clark's death from cause: electrocution; manner: accidental, but we'd best let law enforcement make that decision."

After I call him, Wayne comes by and looks at the mark. I wonder if he'll call the coroner back to take another look or even insist that Amick authorize an autopsy. I leave before he does and spend the afternoon putting signs about Big Boy on telephone poles and in store windows.

As frequently happens, Wayne calls to say he's tied up and won't be able to have dinner with me. Once again, I eat a Quarter Pounder with Cheese with a Moon Pie for dessert. I'm so worried about Big Boy that I can't concentrate on reading, so I watch the movie *Only the Lonely* with John Candy on DVD. I love that movie as much as the old *Six Feet Under* shows.

Wednesday, October 28

Chapter Eleven

THE NEXT MORNING, there are definitely other things I need to do, but all I can think about is trying to find Big Boy. I only had time to post a few signs about Big Boy the day before, so I take the lost-dog notices and head out. Progress is slow because of the constant starting and stopping to post the flyers on utility poles. Downtown, it takes forever as I go in and out of stores. I must say though, that everyone I approach gives me permission to put a sign in the window, and most of them express concern. Several comment that they have friends whose dogs have gone missing also.

As I pass St. Mary High School, I'm surprised that yellow crime scene tape remains across the front door. I drive around to the football field and find that the vacant lot Ty's TEAM class had planned to use for the haunted graveyard is still taped off as well and a canvas tarp covers the hole Ty dug. Beyond the field, I see a tent awning similar to the ones that Middleton's puts over gravesites for interments. I believe campers refer to them as dining tarps. Under it is the man who drives the green Jeep parked on the berm—Bob Everett. The snarky side of me wonders how he managed to get away from Rizzie long enough to come over.

I pull off to the side of the road, stop, and walk over to him. He's so absorbed in what he's doing that I'm right behind him before he realizes I'm here. He's dug out a hole and is sifting soil through a shallow square wooden box with a screen bottom. As he shakes the device carefully, he's also sweeping the dirt back and forth with a small brush.

"What'ya doing?" I ask. Bob Everett sets the box and brush on the ground and wipes his hands on the legs of his cutoff khaki cargo pants. There's a dirt-colored smudge in his beard.

"I'm really eager to see what I can find in that field where Tyrone found the skull," he says and waves toward the taped-off area. "I'm so excited that it will be a real archaeologic find." He grins. "Won't it be something if I discover evidence of another unknown ancient Native American tribe in this area?" He grins even bigger. "I got permission from the owner to work here until law enforcement takes down the tape over there." He motions toward the area surrounded by tape.

"Found anything?" I ask.

"Not really, but I'm not working deep enough to expect much yet. As I dig farther down, I'm hoping to locate artifacts." His eyes light up. "Some of the Native American relics found in South Carolina date back eight thousand years and they've been verified to eleven or twelve hundred A.D."

I'm amazed. I don't know why. It makes sense but I guess I never considered who might have lived here so long ago.

"What kind of artifacts?" I ask.

"Mainly projective points, ceramics, and stone tools so far, but around here is uncharted territory. No telling what I might find when I reach the right location."

"Projective points?" I ask. "Is that another way of saying arrowheads?"

Bob's expression is a little smug. "Yep, I chose to retire to South Carolina because I believe there's more to be discovered here, and I want to be the one who does it. Do you ever have a desire to blaze an uncharted way? Find something nobody's seen before?"

"Not really. I just want to locate my dog."

His expression changes from elation to sympathy. "I hope you have him back soon."

"Thank you." I turn to go back to my car.

"Want to hang around for a while, maybe even help?"

"No, I'm putting up signs about Big Boy."

"Good luck."

I walk a few feet away before he calls me back. "Hey, Callie, will you take a few more minutes and answer a question."

"Sure, what do you want to know?" I ask and step back toward him.

"I'm embarrassed to be asking you this. Makes me feel like a teenager, but then, Rizzie makes me feel like I'm sixteen again." He actually blushes. "We've been seeing each other a lot, and I'm developing strong feelings for her."

"I can understand that," I reply. "Rizzie is a very special lady. What's the question?"

For just a moment, the elderly man resembles a shy adolescent. "Rizzie has seemed special to me since the first time I walked into the grill. She always has a smile for me and never seems too busy to sit down and talk. Like I said, I've developed feelings for her, but I wonder if I'm seeing something that isn't there on her side. Could it just be kindness toward an older newcomer in the neighborhood?"

I laugh. "Rizzie's usually far too busy trying to make a go of the restaurant to sit down and talk to people. I've noticed she joins you more than she's ever sat with me when I go in, and we're longtime friends. Besides, haven't the two of you been to dinner together at other places?"

"Yes, we have. I hadn't thought about that."

"I can't guarantee how Rizzie feels, but I think

she does consider you special." I believe more than that, but I don't want to lead him in the wrong direction, either way.

He opens his mouth as if to respond, then looks pointedly over my shoulder.

"I think," he says, "that there are a couple of admirers for you or that fancy car."

I turn just in time to see the white Econoline pull away. Strange that there's no sign on its side now.

"What do you mean?" I ask.

"That's the third time that van has passed by here since you arrived. It slows down by your car every time. Do you know them?"

"No, but I think I saw that same van the other day with one of those magnetized signs on the side."

"What did it say?"

"Animal Rescue, but it could be a different one."

"Maybe so. Could be a couple of guys infatuated with your Corvette."

"Yes, probably," I say and start to leave, but then I ask, "Will you be working here tomorrow?"

"During the afternoon. In the morning, Rizzie and I are driving to Hilton Head Island. She's never seen the prehistoric shell rings at Skull Island. Some shell rings are three hundred feet in diameter and nine feet high in Georgia. What makes the ones at Skull Island in Carolina unique is that they are the only known ones that have a later ring superimposed over an earlier one."

"What makes that significant?" I ask.

"Well, there are several interpretations of shell rings. Some scientists believe they represent earliest examples of North American year-round occupation. If so, they're essentially trash heaps where individuals dumped things. Another theory is that they were seasonally occupied camps where ceremonies and feasts were held. If that's true, the rings were made by people intentionally piling up the remains of feasts, possibly for some spiritual meaning. Then there are archaeologists who think the rings resulted from both feasts and from year-round occupation of the sites. Rings on top of previous ones shows people were there during two different eras."

To me, he sounds like a Wikipedia article. Archaeology doesn't interest me much, but skulls do since my fall at the Halsey house and Ty's find in the adjacent field.

"Skull Island?" I ask. "Are these rings made out of skulls?"

Bob Everett laughs. "If there are skulls in there, they're crushed. The rings, or middens as they're called, are circular and semicircular deposits with a high concentration of oyster shells. They also contain bone, soil, and artifacts including some of the earliest pottery ever found in North America—as far back as the end of the Late Archaic Period around three thousand years ago."

"Whew," I exclaim. Sounds like shell rings could be dumps and this man is a walking info dump. "Too educational for me," I say. "Are you sure Rizzie is interested in all this?"

"We started talking about Gullah history, and now she seems curious about my Native American studies as well." His expression is so sad and unhappy that I feel sorry for him even before he asks, "You don't think she's just being kind, do you?"

"If she's just being nice, she must care enough about you to be making the effort. But I'll tell you this: Rizzie is a busy, busy lady, and if she wasn't genuinely interested, I don't think she'd pretend to be. Besides, Rizzie hardly ever takes time off from work. That should tell you something."

"Would you like to go with us to Skull Island?" he asks.

"No, I think I'll be tied up at the mortuary all day tomorrow."

WHEN I REACH WORK, I begin preparing for the Clark visitation. My responsibilities include seeing that the room is properly set up as well as ordering flowers and food, which I've already handled.

Recent renovations at Middleton's enable us to combine several slumber rooms into one big reception hall. Otis and Odell have moved the portable dividing walls before I arrive, making the area as large as possible for Mr. Clark's visitation. Some people think the term "visitation" refers to coming to see the person who died. The "visiting" part is to socialize and express sympathy to the survivors, so the fact that Mr. Clark wound up on his way to Charleston for a postmortem exam after the sheriff came by the night before has no bearing on the Gray Lady's reception for her brother, whom I've begun to think of as the Gray Man after I dressed him.

A lot of the time Otis and Odell call in part-timers to set up chairs and tables, but they're doing it themselves this morning.

If I say so myself, when we finish, the room looks as beautiful as I've ever seen it. Ms. Clark gave permission to spend whatever was necessary for it to be "nice for Norm." I ordered white rose arrangements for the food tables as well as for both sides of the sixty-inch television on which the memorial video is looped to repeat itself over and over. The bluegrass gospel she selected makes me miss my father. He would love the selections. If Miss Ellen didn't have him off on another cruise, I could have made Ms. Clark's day by having Daddy and my brothers perform live.

When Ms. Clark asked for sandwiches and petit fours, I thought nineteen-fifties. I guess my thoughts went there because my mind hadn't moved beyond the concept of that flashback 1959 prom reunion. She called me after Wayne let her know there would be an autopsy, after all.

"Miss Parrish, this is Eva Clark. Did you know that they decided to send Norm to Charleston to see how he died even though we know his hot tub killed him? I've heard there's some talk about me wanting him cremated because it's cheaper, but that's not the reason at all. I want him cremated because he loved fire and so I can keep his ashes at my house. I've been reading, too, that you can have the ashes put into tattoos so the dead person is always with you. Do y'all do that?"

"No, ma'am. We don't do tattoos, but you will receive the cremains and can do whatever you like so long as you don't break the law."

"What do you mean, break the law?"

"Well, there are certain places that you won't be allowed to spread ashes. One of them is that they can't be dropped from commercial airplanes." I thought for a moment. "We do have some literature about various ways to keep the cremains close to you. One of them is to have some of them sealed in a locket. It comes in silver or gold."

"Will all of the cremains fit?"

"Oh, no, ma'am. Cremains for a grown man will be about six pounds. You would have only a small amount put in the locket. You could scatter the rest or keep them in a special urn."

"I'd like to see the literature on a locket when I come back in. That tattoo business sounds loving, but I have an idea getting it done would hurt. Do you have any tattoos, Ms. Parrish?"

"No, ma'am. I'll give you some brochures about cremains jewelry when you come for the visitation."

"That's what I called about. Since some folks think I'm trying to save money, I want to make this visitation absolutely spectacular. Mr. Middleton said you will be the one who places the orders and I should talk to you about it."

Now, back when I was thinking fifties, I ordered pimento cheese, cream cheese and olive, and chicken salad sandwiches for the Clark visitation. All sandwiches to be cut into quarters and the crusts removed. The only reason I didn't order egg salad was because it doesn't always smell good. Heck! Get a bunch of men in here eating egg salad, and the room wouldn't smell so good either. Now I'm thinking maybe she'll change to more modern refreshments, but instead she says, "I want you to be sure we have little dishes of mints and nuts set around, and I'd like silver and crystal serving dishes. Can you do that?"

I assure her it will all be first class, and now, looking at the silver trays lined with doilies, I know Ms. Clark will be pleased. I made one additional change on my own. She insisted on a chip and dip tray, but now instead of just onion dip, the large crystal punch bowl filled with chips is surrounded by an assortment of little dishes containing clam, shrimp, and avocado dips as well as the onion.

I can hardly wait for Ms. Clark to arrive and see how gorgeous everything is. The delay isn't very long. "It Is No Secret" announces someone's arrival. I meet Ms. Clark in the front hall, and I'm not surprised to see she's wearing a gray dress. I lead her to the visitation room and have the pleasure of seeing her gasp with delight.

"It's classy," she says. "Exactly what I want. Where do I stand when the people start coming?"

Since she's the only family member, there won't be a receiving line. "You may stand wherever you like," I say, "but I suggest over here by the guest book." She's delighted with the podium and register, which were my idea, as well as the white rose in a crystal bud vase beside the book.

The announcement on our webpage and in the newspaper invited visitors to come at three o'clock, but the room is full by two-forty-five. I recognize many of the townspeople as well as my brothers John, Bill, Mike, and Frank. My fifth brother Jim lives in New York, so he isn't here. I assume Mrs. Barnes left immediately following Melvin Barnes's interment the day before, which explains why she's missing.

Sammy Bee, actually Samuel Blevins, but everyone calls him Sammy Bee because that's what he named his car lot, is in the corner talking to Wayne and Fletcher Williams. Fletcher is wobbling a bit, and Wayne reaches out to steady him. Fletcher yanks back and screeches, "Don't touch me. I told them I didn't do anything. I'm not guilty. Don't you arrest me."

Paranoia, I think. *Probably brought on by his excessive drinking.*

I'm glad to be across the room with Odell between me and the corner where they are. He joins Wayne and Mr. Blevins as they try to calm Fletcher. The men walk the inebriated man from the room just as they did at the reunion.

When Wayne and Sammy return, I notice Allie heading toward them. Like Saturday night, she's wearing red and dressed to attract attention, though her outfit is business attire: a fitted skirt suit with a snug, lacy, cream-colored camisole peeking from beneath the jacket at her neck. Naturally she has on another pair of red high heels.

Call it silly or not, but regardless of how she acts around me, I'm not sure if Allie is my friend when it comes to Wayne. In fact, I'm not sure if Alice Lara Patterson is a real friend to any other woman who has a male friend. I hike myself over to where they're standing before Allie turns my eyes green with the way she's looking up at Wayne as he answers a question. When I arrive, she nods at me and then turns her attention to Sammy Bee.

"I've decided to stay in St. Mary for a while and write my book. It's ridiculous to keep renting a car. Could you fix me up with something reliable and fairly reasonable, Sammy?"

The car salesman expression spreads over Sam Blevins's face like glaze over a Krispy Kreme doughnut. "Of course, Alice. Ask Callie here. She bought that gorgeous yellow baby she drives from us. Would you like to come by the lot and take a look when this is over?"

"No, I have an appointment to meet a rental agent at Hidden Lake to look at the cabins when I leave here. Living in a B & B if I'm staying in St. Mary doesn't make any more sense than renting a car."

"You're right, and I understand that the owners are remodeling and refurnishing some of the lodgings at the lake. I've heard they're real nice," Sammy says. "Do you think you'll eventually move into your family home place?"

"All I've done for years is pay taxes on it, and I haven't been out to look at the property yet. For all I know, the house and barns may have fallen down by now."

Wayne interrupts, "Don't go out there looking around by yourself. Callie fell through a rotten step at the old Halsey place just last Saturday." He gets that concerned look on his face. I'm familiar with it because he directs it at me when he thinks I might do something dangerous. I don't like him looking at Allie like that even if he is the sheriff and part of his job is to serve and protect all St. Mary citizens.

Sure enough, Allie asks, "Could you go with me to check it out one day, Wayne?"

"Let me know when you're ready to go there," Wayne says, and I bristle until he adds, "and I'll send one of the deputies with you."

"Or I could go," Sammy says.

"Don't you have to work?" Allie asks with a hint of flirtation in her voice.

Sammy Bee's chest puffs up as he tells her, "I make my own hours. I *own* the car lot." He grins and asks, "When do you want to testdrive some transportation?"

I can't help but wonder if Sammy's offer to go with Allie to look at cabins has any significance beyond just ingratiating himself with her in hopes of selling her a car.

"Tomorrow morning will be good," Allie says. She looks at me, "Want to go with me?"

"I have to be at work by ten," I answer.

"Tell you what," Sammy Bee says. "We open at nine o'clock, but if you girls want, I'll come in early. Meet me at my car lot at eight, and I'll show you the best cars before anyone else arrives. Come around to the back of the building. I'll be in my office and will have the sliding glass doors unlocked."

Allie's face lights up. Shopping for a car was fun when I bought my Corvette, but I'm not overly excited about looking at vehicles with her. On the other hand, Sammy Bee's a married man whose youngest child Zack is a friend of Tyrone's. I decide to go just to protect Ty's buddy from some kind of mess like Melvin Barnes got into with his wife at the reunion. I'd like to say that I'm sure Sammy's only interest is to sell a car, but I remember something my daddy told me long ago: "Callie, there's a little bit of dog in a lot of men."

Allie and I agree that I'll pick her up from the B & B at seven the next morning and stop for coffee on the way. I notice she departs without ever going over to express her condolences to Norman Clark's sister.

When the Clark visitation ends, Wayne leaves without mentioning seeing me later. I stay to help clean up.

"Ms. Parrish, I can't thank you enough," the Gray Lady gushes before she exits with boxes of leftover food from the caterer—just like the bride and groom leaving from a wedding reception, except that it's much sadder. Ms. Clark is also carrying a handful of brochures about ways to use her brother's cremains along with some sandwiches and petit fours.

While Otis and I set things back in order, taking down tables and chairs, Odell comes in supporting Fletcher Williams beside him and says, "I'm taking Fletch home. He's been sleeping it off on the love seat in the Magnolia Room."

"He looks like he's sleep walking," I comment looking at the man's drooping head and closed eyes.

"Drive him home in the funeral coach," Otis suggests.

I don't know if Odell will do that or not, but if

he does, I'd love to see Fletcher Williams when he realizes he's riding in a hearse

WAYNE HAS PROPOSED MARRIAGE several times, but I'm not ready for a twenty-four-hour, seven-days-a-week relationship. I really have no interest in seeing another man, but I don't even want to live together, much less get married. My first (and so far only) marriage ended in an ugly divorce. I have to be absolutely, one hundred percent positive the next time.

Tonight, at home alone in bed, I miss having Big Boy on the floor beside me, and I guess if I'm being truthful, I miss spooning with Wayne. He's not a really big man, but all snuggled in his arms, I feel as protected as if he were seven feet tall and bulletproof.

In the past, if I felt lonely, I called Jane and we got together. It wasn't uncommon for one of us to run next door to the other's apartment in the middle of the night. Usually I went to her place because while I normally have Moon Pies in my cupboard, Jane loves to bake and most of the time, she has homemade sticky buns or cinnamon rolls. Now I don't call and go over in the wee hours because Frankie is there a lot, and whether he is or not, since she's slowed down working as Roxanne, I'm afraid she'll be sleeping if I call. I could really go for some homemade goodies. I can almost taste some of the delicious treats Jane and I used to share in the middle of the night, but I eat the last Moon Pie in the apartment. I'll definitely go shopping tomorrow.

Thursday, October 29

Chapter Twelve

WHEN MORNING ARRIVES, it feels strange to wake up and not need to let Big Boy into the yard for his morning business, but I get a quick shower and dress in khakis and a brown sweater. I take a black dress, stockings, and heels for work out to the car in a garment bag. I'll change when I get to the mortuary.

Allie meets me at the door of the B & B. She's cut her hair shorter and lightened it another shade. I notice she hasn't been totally successful with the color. It's darker around her ears, almost green, but she's smiling and in a good mood. She tells me, "I rented the cutest cabin yesterday afternoon. You'll have to come see it. I'm moving in this evening."

The B & B proprietor offers us French toast to go with our coffee. Sitting at the table, we can see across the counter to the kitchen. She cuts off two slices from a French loaf and stuffs peach preserves between them before the traditional dipping in egg mixture with cinnamon and frying in butter. A sprinkle of confectioners' sugar over the top, and it's scrumptious without even adding syrup.

As we eat, Allie teases about buying a pickup truck and moving out to the farm. She's laughing and fun. I feel a wee bit guilty for my jealousy and suspicions of Allie the previous day. When we go out to the parking lot, Allie pats the hood of my Vette with the affection I reserve for Big Boy. Although the air is crisp and cool, Allie asks, "Can we put the top down?"

We ride through St. Mary giggling, carrying on like schoolgirls, and enjoying the breeze in our hair. Allie's color is really bad. I may offer to help her get that green tinge out after all. When we reach Sammy Bee's Cream of the Crop Autos, the night lights are still on. I'm happy to see that the car in the main showroom is exactly like mine.

"Pull around back," Allie says. "He said to go in through his office door."

At the rear of the building, a sleek, black, top-of-the-line Camaro is backed up close to the glass of the sliding doors. I park beside it before I notice the Camaro's engine is running.

"He must have just arrived," I say as I get out of the Vette.

I walk over to the back of the car, planning to

knock on the glass door. That's when I see it.

Attached to the exhaust of the Camaro with duct tape is a piece of flexible ductwork like what's used to vent my clothes dryer at the apartment. It leads to the glass where even more tape has been used to seal around a hole in the sliding glass door entry into the building.

Allie stands motionless beside me gasping. I push on the sliding glass door to open it, but it won't budge.

"Turn off the car's ignition," I shout, open the trunk of my car, and grab the tire jack.

Allie tries to undo the driver's door of the Camaro, but turns around and says, "I can't. It's locked."

I swing the jack against the sliding door and am happy that the glass shatters. Using the tool to knock away the jagged edges, I reach inside and unfasten the door.

Tossing the jack back to Allie, I tell her, "Use this to break the window and cut off the engine."

Sammy Bee sits at a stunningly elegant, dark walnut desk that's about six feet wide. His head is nestled into his folded arms on the glass-topped surface. Mr. Blevins's face is cherry pink as though he's blushing at his own thoughts.

A family photo framed in brushed stainless steel shows him with his wife and their three children. The two older kids are both girls and look college-age. The youngest is Zack though the picture isn't recent. The teenager is wearing regular clothing and Justin Beiber hair.

"Open those doors all the way and help me," I scream at Allie as I grab the man under his arms. Together, we tug him to the floor and drag him from his office into the showroom. I slam the door behind us and tell her, "Call 911." I begin CPR though I've been working at the mortuary long enough to know that Sammy Bee has sold his last car.

When the EMTs and deputies arrive, I'm disappointed that Wayne isn't with them. I ask and am told he'll probably be there soon.

Allie has collapsed in hysterical sobs. "This is too much," she cries, "too much. People are dying all the time."

I can't help it. I say, "Every day."

One of the ambulance guys insists on checking Allie's pulse. He thinks both of us probably inhaled enough carbon monoxide to warrant some oxygen, but I decline. I just want to sit on the expensive upholstered couch in the showroom and see what Wayne says about Sammy Bee's death. I'm sure the coroner will call it suicide, but the desk top was clear except for the family photograph. There was no note. Don't suicidal people usually leave something in writing? Three of four close high school friends have died in the past week. Two of them mighr be by suicide. Coincidental? Wayne says that cops don't believe in coincidence. What will he say about this?

No Wayne, but employees begin arriving. The manager announces the business will be closed for the day, so salesmen and service people are dismissed.

Allie and I both give our statements to the deputies. Coroner Amick comes, examines the scene and the body, and pronounces Sammy Bee's death as suicide. Odell arrives in the removal van.

"Callie, why don't you take a few hours off? Actually, just take the day off. Otis and I will cover everything."

"What about Mr. Blevins? Won't you need me to take him to Charleston to be examined or to be at the funeral home when Mrs. Blevins comes in?" I ask.

"I'll send a part-timer over to take chairs and registers to the Blevins home later this evening. She doesn't even know her husband's deceased yet. I'll try to schedule the planning session for tomorrow at eleven. I'll definitely want you there around ten in the morning."

As Allie and I get into the Vette, Wayne finally arrives.

"Where have you been?" I ask as though I have any business questioning the sheriff. I'm not certain that I have a right as a girlfriend when he's off duty, but I *know* I'm out of line questioning his whereabouts when he's working.

"As a matter of fact, I was at the Blevins home taking information from Mrs. Blevins because she wanted to file a missing person report. Sammy didn't go home last night. I confess I went to assure her that even though he hadn't been gone long enough to make it official, I would look into it myself. I was planning to head over here even before I learned what happened. I wanted to talk to Sammy, but that's not going to happen."

He looks at me. "I guess you found the body, Callie?"

"Don't say 'body.' We call the deceased by his name."

"That's how you and the Middletons refer to them. I call dead people the bodies or corpses."

For the first time, he seems to notice Allie.

"Hello, Alice. I'm sure you weren't expecting this. I guess it was quite a surprise."

"Yes, I came to buy a car. I can't believe how it turned out."

Wayne doesn't respond to her comment, but says, "I understand a deputy took your statements. I'll read over them and let you know if I have additional questions."

I want to ask him about there not being a suicide note, but one of the deputies calls him. He walks away, and I pull out of the parking spot.

"Do you want to go anywhere before I take you back to the B & B?" I ask.

"Would you mind going to a store with me to pick up a few things?"

"No, I won't mind. Where do you want to go?"

"The cabin is furnished, but I'll need linens

and kitchen things. We could go to a nice department store, but if I decide not to stay, I don't want to take a bunch of things with me. Let's just go to Walmart." She laughs. "If I decide to stay indefinitely or move into the farm, I can buy more permanent items then."

"Wally-World, it is." I say.

A couple of hours later, we put the top up on the Vette so we can lock it. Not that a canvas top is going to stop a thief from stealing what's in a car, but it should be a visual deterrent if not a physical one. Into the car, we load a set of bedsheets, pillows and cases, a blanket, a sixteen-piece set of Corelle dishes, a sixteen-piece set of flatware, an inexpensive set of cookware, a coffeepot, small slow-cooker, broom, and mop.

"Well, that should get me started," Allie says.

"I can't think of any other immediate needs," I comment. "You can pick up soap, dish detergent, and that kind of stuff when you buy groceries. Where to now?"

"Do you want to ride out and see the cabin?" Allie asks.

"Later," I answer and drive to the B & B. We unload everything into her rental car. She looks so forlorn that I feel sad for her and suggest, "Want to have lunch before you drive out to Hidden Lake to start housekeeping?"

Allie's eyes light up. I suggest we go to Gastric Gullah Grill and begin giving her directions.

"That's kind of on the way to Hidden Lake.

173

Why don't I follow you to the restaurant, and then I'll drive on out to the cabin from there."

When I pull into Rizzie's parking lot, I wish I'd mentioned going somewhere else. Both Bob Everett's Jeep and Frankie's truck are here. I'm even more surprised that they're sitting together, but then I see Rizzie and Ty behind the counter, and I assume Jane's in the kitchen. Bob waves at me and invites us to join them.

"Oh, no," I protest, "Rizzie or Jane might want to sit with you."

"They're both busy and will stay that way through lunchtime. Jane is busy cooking, and the server didn't come in," Frankie offers.

I perform introductions and ask, "What's the special today?"

"Jane's trying one of the recipes submitted for her cookbook," Frankie says. "A lady named Jen Stallings emailed it to her right after the notice was posted on the grill's website. Jane made it at home before cooking it here. It's really good."

"What's it called?" Allie asks.

"Pastitsio," Frankie says. "It's a Greek pasta dish."

Right then, Ty comes to the table for our orders. We all request sweet iced tea and the special.

When Ty walks away, I ask Bob, "Are you and Rizzie back from Skull Island already?"

"Decided to wait and go tomorrow," he answers. "Has the sheriff mentioned those skulls?

I'd hoped I have the chance to examine them, but I haven't heard from him."

Once again, I tell him Wayne doesn't often share what's happening professionally with me. Allie inserts, "He's probably too busy with the deaths and missing dogs right now."

"Missing dogs?" Frankie asks. "Did you say plural of dog? I knew Big Boy got out of the fence, but I didn't know anything about other dogs."

Tyrone returns with the teas just in time to hear the word "dogs."

"Did you say something about hot dogs?" he asks Frankie.

"No, we're talking about dogs being missing or stolen," I say and take a sip of tea.

"I overheard them talking about a dog-theft ring at the B & B," Allie says. "Seems like more dogs are disappearing every night."

I make a mental note to call and ask Wayne about it as soon as I get away from the others. Ty leaves and comes back with four small salads. I see that Jane's going with the Greek origin of the special by adding calamata olives, peppers, and feta cheese to the salads. Each plate has a piece of fresh-baked bread on it.

"What do you mean the deaths may be keeping him busy?" Bob Everett asks. "Those two accidental deaths wouldn't tie up law enforcement all that much."

"I heard the same people talking about there being some confusion whether the school principal's death was accident or suicide," Allie says and before anyone comments, she adds, "And then, I don't guess you know, but Sammy Bee committed suicide last night in his office at his car lot."

"What?" Frankie's tone is as shocked as the expression on his face. "Why would he do that? Did he leave a note explaining why?"

"Not that we know of," I say.

"Don't tell me you found the body," Frankie says to me.

"Actually, we both did," Allie says. "I went in early to buy a car, and we found him."

"How did he do it?" Bob asks.

"Carbon monoxide poisoning," I answer him.

"Thought you said he died in his office," Frankie says.

"Had the back end of his Camaro connected to a hole he must have made in the sliding glass doors to his office," Allie says. "There was no note."

"Or at least we didn't see a note," I add. "He may have left something in a desk drawer or somewhere else."

"I didn't think about looking," Allie says.

"I wouldn't have let you if you'd wanted to," I say. "The sheriff would be furious if we touched anything looking for a note. Technically, we shouldn't have moved the body, but I felt we had to just in case he wasn't all the way gone. It would have been stupid to stay in his office."

At that moment, Rizzie approaches balancing four plates on her arms. She sets one in front of each of us. The entrees smell tantalizing and are cut into squares like lasagna, but instead of flat pasta, I can see this is something similar to elbow macaroni and has a white sauce as well as meat. One forkful and I agree with Frankie. This is an excellent use of ground meat. I'm sure it will make it into Jane's cookbook. I can't cook worth anything, but sometimes I'm pretty good identifying ingredients. I just always seem to foul up quantities, even when I follow recipes. This has a slight edge I can't identify, but it's really tasty.

"You know, suicide used to have a greater social stigma than it does now," Allie comments between bites. "Churches wouldn't allow people who committed suicide to be buried in their graveyards." She coughs and then continues, "Even the terminology is prejudicial. People don't 'do' suicide; they 'commit' it like a crime."

"And yet in some cultures, suicide is a noble thing to do. In ancient Rome, it was an honorable death," Bob says. "And don't forget those suicide terrorist bombers. Suicide is a lot like capital punishment—thought wrong in some places, praised in others."

"Isn't the United States the only country that still uses capital punishment and that's only in some states?" Allie asks.

"No, it's less prevalent than it used to be, but

it's not solely confined to parts of America," Bob says. "Throughout history, people have been beheaded both on a chopping block and by guillotine, hanged both publicly and privately, shot by firing squad, died in gas chambers, been electrocuted, even drawn and quartered before the current method of lethal injection was implemented."

"Was execution always for murder?" Allie asks.

"In the past, execution was punishment for many, many crimes including adultery, rape, and theft, as well as witchcraft." He pauses a moment before adding, "And especially for treason."

I can't resist asking, "How do you know all that? It's history, but that's not part of your specialty in archeology, is it?"

"Not really, but all history intrigues me, and I've had a special interest in capital punishment since I did a report about it way back when I was a teenager." He pauses. "Oh, I left out burning at the stake which involved setting fire to living people."

I shiver in revulsion. "Please," I say, "let's change the subject. I deal with death every day, but this creeps me out."

Allie ignores me and asks Bob, "Of all that, what do you think is the most cruel method?"

"Drawn and quartered," Bob says and uses a piece of bread to wipe up the sauce left on his plate after the last bite and looks at me. "Are you familiar with that?"

"No," we answer together.

"Sometimes drawn and quartered followed hanging and disemboweling, but at times, it was the method of death itself. A person was tied to four horses, one attached to each arm and leg, and then the horses were whipped into a frenzy. The horses ran off in opposite directions, resulting in the body being torn apart into four pieces." This man is a walking encyclopedia.

I grimace. This conversation is too horrible for me to think about, especially just after eating.

"What do you think, Callie?" Allie asks. "Do you support capital punishment?"

"Cinnamon," I say.

"Cinnamon?" Allie questions.

"That's the taste I couldn't identify."

"Yes," Bob says, "there's a touch of cinnamon in pastitsio."

"Oh," Allie says softly before she repeats the question, "Callie, do you support capital punishment?" Before I can answer, she adds, "I sure do."

"That's hard to answer," I say and pause as Ty refills tea glasses before stopping to listen to my answer. "I'm not generally in favor of putting anyone to death by any means, yet when I think of the two most famous executions in South Carolina, I can see where the families of their victims would support it."

"Who were the last two in South Carolina?" Ty

asks.

Bob answers for me. "Pee Wee Gaskins went to the electric chair in 1991, convicted of killing nine people, but confessed to killing over one hundred people. Larry Gene Bell was executed in 1996, convicted of kidnapping and murdering teenager Shari Smith and nine-year-old Debra May Helmick. He called their relatives and verbally tormented them before giving both families the locations of their daughters' remains. For years, Bell was known as the 'last person electrocuted' in this state, but since then James Earl Reed chose to die in Old Sparky in 2008. Reed's crime was killing his ex-girlfriend's parents, and it happened in Adams Run, not far from here."

"Old Sparky?" Allie asks.

"Chose?" I ask.

"Both Bell and Reed were allowed to choose between lethal injection and South Carolina's electric chair which was called Old Sparky. They each chose the electric chair."

"I just want to know your personal feelings," Allie insists, looking directly at me.

"Me personally?" I answer. "I'm really on the fence about capital punishment. Some people commit crimes that I think are so horrendous that they don't deserve a life. They don't deserve to be fed, clothed, and maintained with medical attention, but then I think about those cases where someone who isn't guilty is convicted.

There's no turning back after a person is executed if the court gets it wrong.

"So, based on that," I continue, "I'm against it, but I think if someone murdered or even worse, did some of the horrific crimes involving torture to someone I love, I think I might be in favor of executing the person who did it."

Frankie speaks up. "I'm even more callous than Callie. If someone did some of the things I read about and see on the news to Jane or Callie, I'd want that person executed and I wouldn't care a whole lot about it being painless."

"What about you, Bob?" Allie asks.

"No way," he says. "I don't believe in it at all. For society to take a life and call it legal reduces our country to the same level as the criminal."

I may not have a definite opinion on capital punishment, but I do know that while Bob Everett's always polite, he would get on my nerves constantly sounding like he's teaching in a classroom. Rizzie must care a lot about him to put up with his incessant instruction.

Chapter Thirteen

ANYONE WHO THINKS THIS BOOK has a thirteenth chapter is wrong, wrong, wrong. When I lived in Columbia, I went into tall buildings that didn't have thirteenth floors. The elevators went from the eleventh floor to the fourteenth. Friday, the thirteenth, is bad luck. Because of these and other associations of the number thirteen with doom, I refuse to write a Chapter Thirteen.

Chapter Fourteen

"COME ON, CALLIE. You said you're not going back to work. Go with us to Skull Creek. It's near Hilton Head, and the trip won't take long—three hours max. Less than an hour there, an hour or so to see the shell rings, and less than an hour back. I'll pack a picnic lunch for an early dinner on the way home."

"Rizzie, I need to go out and look for Big Boy."

"We hardly ever have any time together. Go with us." She fakes a pout and then smiles. "I *really* want you to."

BOB EVERETT'S JEEP GRAND CHEROKEE is a comfortable ride, and we talk all the way from St. Mary to near Hilton Head, but the topic is mainly about Native Americans and history, and the speaker is Bob Everett. Rizzie does better at paying attention than I do. I wonder why.

"Combined, the shell rings on the coasts of Georgia and South Carolina number about twenty with the ones at Skull Creek being two of them," Bob Everett drones on.

I let Rizzie talk me into coming on this trip, but my mind is on Big Boy. I'm wishing I'd stayed back in St. Mary and broadened my search for him.

"Glad you ladies wore your walking shoes," Bob Everett continues, "because we can't drive up to the shell rings. We'll have to park and walk in."

Rizzie asks polite questions between my uh-huh's, but I drift off into my own thoughts, and though they are mostly about Big Boy, the deaths of three men who were friends since childhood seems far too much to be coincidental. That is, unless Sammy Bee's suicide was triggered by the loss of the other two.

We've been on the road about forty-five minutes when Mother Nature notifies me she'd like to make a call. "Bathroom break," I say.

Only a few minute later, Bob Everett pulls into the parking lot of a fairly small strip mall. Rizzie and I visit the ladies' room at a coffee shop and are headed back to the Jeep when I notice a little store with the front window draped in black. A mannequin dressed in exactly the same clothing Ty's friend Zack wore at the haunted graveyard site is the only decoration in the window. The figure holds a sign with creepy letters spelling out

Skull Creek Goth Shop

"Let's go in there," I suggest to Rizzie.

"What for?" Rizzie asks. "Thought you wanted to get back fairly early."

"I won't stay long. Just want to look around."

Whenever the front door opens at the mortuary, instrumental hymns and gospel songs play. When we step into the Skull Creek Goth Shop, I hear a recorded loud, creaking sound. Hung with prints and paintings of skulls, ravens, and gothic castles, the walls are draped in black cloth making it impossible to identify an entrance or exit behind the counter. In less than a minute, the fabric parts and a woman steps through. Wearing a floor-length, deep burgundy velvet dress with a brocade bodice and long, bat-wing sleeves, she's tall and thin with gray-streaked hair falling down her back, far too long for a female her age. I assume the darkness around her barbiturate eyes is makeup and that some of the hollowness of her cheeks is careful contouring. When she gestures toward us, I notice that she has rings on every finger—not jewels but metallic goblins and raven-shaped carvings.

"May I help you?" she asks in a low voice.

"I noticed your shop and wanted to look around." I glance at the shelves. Almost everything on display is skull-shaped—incense burners, candle holders, key chains, and other small items—but no life-size skulls.

"Are you tourists?" the clerk asks.

"Not really," Rizzie answers. "We're from St. Mary."

"I thought your accents were local—a little Geechee there." The saleslady looks directly into Rizzie's eyes and suggests, "Perhaps someone sent you to the Goth Shop for a particular item?" She grins. "What you see are the items we sell to tourists as souvenirs. We have lots of additional merchandise in the back." She stares at Rizzie even harder during her last statement.

"What kind of special memento would you recommend?" Rizzie asks.

"This can opener is nice." The woman, who I now think of as Morticia, picks up a mechanical opener with a skull where the can will fit. It's clever since the upper and lower teeth close to clamp whatever is being opened. "Most people have electric ones, but mechanical is good to have when the power is out." She holds it up and shows us that the skull's lower jaw opens to grasp the can by snapping it open and closed.

When Rizzie nor I comment, she sets the opener down and motions toward the pictures on the wall. "Each of these is for sale as well," she says. "And, as I said, I have a lot more in the back—black candles, potions, mojo bags and ingredients. All you have to do is tell me what you want."

On impulse, I say, "I want a skull, a human skull." As the words leave my mouth, I feel something against my leg. It's eerie and just a tad bit frightening until I look down and see a small cat—a black cat, of course.

"Lucifer!" the clerk scolds the animal before turning her attention toward Rizzie and me. "He usually stays in back." She picks up the half-grown cat and places him on her shoulder.

Morticia says, "Skulls are no problem," and reaches beneath the counter. She brings out a clean, white, life-size human skull. I reach for it, and she puts it in my hand. I can feel that it's made of some type of plastic.

"No," I say and hand it back. "I want something more realistic."

She brings another one from beneath the counter. It looks more authentic.

"This is top-of-the-line," she says, and I see the difference. This one could pass for real.

"How much?" I ask.

Her answer knocks me back mentally. She quotes a dollar amount far higher than my purse can produce.

"What's it made of?" I ask.

"High quality plastic. The cost is due to the hand painting." She brushes her fingertips across the top of it, almost as though she's caressing the skull. "Do you want it?"

"No." The price is too high, but I'm not really planning to *buy* a skull. I just want more information from her. I can't help but wonder if the skull beneath the stairway at the Halsey house is something similar to this. Mr. Douglas said it was real, but I have no idea how much he knows about old bones.

"What if someone wanted a genuine, real human skull?" I ask. "Could you supply that?"

Before she answers, the door opens and Bob Everett enters. "What are you ladies doing?" he asks.

"Callie was asking if she has any real human skulls for sale," Rizzie answers.

"I told her I don't," the clerk says and shakes her head back and forth.

"Oh, that's not impossible to get," Bob says. "They sell them on the Internet as medical supplies. Why do you want one, Callie?"

"I thought perhaps the skull we found at the Halsey house came from somewhere like this."

"Your boyfriend seems to think it may be from a homicide, but I suspect it's someone practicing some kind of voodoo or witchcraft using a skull bought from the Internet or a store like this, maybe even from this very shop. The reason I want to get my hands on it is there's a very slim chance that it was found around St. Mary and is of archaeological value."

"I've never sold anything I suspected was legitimately human or of historical significance," the clerk says. "But I do sell a ton of fake skulls. People who shop here decorate with them."

"Then why don't you have a lot of them on display?" Rizzie asks.

"People will pay more if they think they're getting something special, something that's not on exhibit out here for everyone to purchase. They feel special and want unique items. I don't tell them that whatever I show them is the only one I have, but it's not my fault if that's what they think."

"Well, thank you for your time," Bob says to her in a dismissive tone and then asks us, "Are you ladies ready to go?"

As we turn to leave, I see it and can't believe I didn't notice it before. To the right of the door is a small table. On it sits a skull with red paper poppies lying around it and a few projecting from the openings.

"What's that?" I point to the display. "Does it have to do with the Veterans of Foreign Wars or American Legion? They use crepe paper poppies on Memorial Day."

"Yes, they do. Red poppies are used to remember the fallen of various wars and armed conflicts, but this has nothing to do with that," Morticia says. "Poppies are symbols of rebirth, consolation, peace in death, and lots of other thoughts related to resurrection and eternal life. That arrangement of a skull with poppies is related to messages delivered in dreams. The practitioner believes that sleeping near a skull with poppies around it leads to spiritual contact through dreams." She pauses and again stares at Rizzie. "Would you like to buy the display?"

"Not the whole thing," I answer, "but I would like a couple of the paper flowers. Can I get a few of those?"

"Don't tell anyone because I'm here to make money, but I'll *give* you some of them. I have plenty more in back." She picks up three of the poppies and hands them to me.

When we're back on the road, I ask Bob, "Did you know all that stuff about poppies?"

"No, I've never heard of putting poppies with a skull to facilitate spiritual communication during sleep, but the sleep part may be related to the poppy's relationship to opium."

"It's not Gullah. I can tell you that," Rizzie says. She giggles. "Did either of you see how she kept staring at me?"

Bob and I both acknowledged noticing.

"She realized I'm Gullah and thought I would be more likely to buy something than either of you."

"Profiling?" I ask.

"Prejudice," Bob says.

We continue to Skull Creek near Hilton Head Island.

When we arrive at the designated parking area to see the shell rings, a sign announces, WALKING TRAFFIC ONLY. NO MOTORIZED VEHICLES OR HORSES. Bob knows all about the place and leads Rizzie and me through beautiful marsh land. When he announces, "Ta-da!" and points, Rizzie's eyes widen, and it's obvious she's delighted. I see he's pointing to a big pile of what looks like crushed oyster shells over a hundred and twenty feet in diameter and over seven feet tall in places. *What a humongous dump!* I think. *Did we come all this way for that?*

I'm sorry but I'm not as impressed as Bob obviously thinks Rizzie and I should be. She, on the other hand, appears totally captivated. The next thing I know, they're holding hands and wandering around looking at the ring from various positions. I'm not inclined to walk with them, and I can't help checking my watch every few minutes.

When they finally come back to me, I ask as lightly as I can manage, "About ready to go? I'm getting hungry."

That's when Rizzie makes this big to-do that she forgot the picnic. Bob says, "No big deal. I will treat you ladies to a meal almost as good as your picnic supper would have been." He clears his throat. "I'm afraid that Callie didn't enjoy this as much as you and I, Rizzie." He glances over his shoulder back at me. "What's your most favorite seafood, Callie?"

"Probably Rizzie's special combination Po Boy sandwich with Cajun-seasoned fried shrimp on one end and oysters on the other."

"I mean something you can't always get at Gastric Gullah Grill."

"I'm partial to soft-shelled crabs, but they're not in season, and I don't like them frozen."

"Well, we're in for a treat. Right off the island is one of my favorite seafood restaurants. I'll guarantee it's not like the other seafood places in this area."

Bob stops at a free-standing building that I would never have considered and driven right past. It's what I've always thought of as "a hole in the wall" with a sign in the window revealing that we're at Gordon's Seafood. The inside is small with a case across the back filled with ice, fish, and other seafood.

To the left of the front door are three small, rickety-looking tables with four equally wobbly-looking chairs pulled up to each one. Men in casual clothes including those hats with fancy fishing lures stuck in them sit at one table. The other two are empty. On the right of the room, two older women in aprons tend a small kitchen area. One of them is scaling fish; the other is watching grease bubble in a fryer.

"Hi, Martha and Ethel," Bob Everett calls to the females. "Ladies, allow me to introduce everyone. These are my friends Rizzie and Callie." He points to each of us. "Martha is the one scaling those flounder and Ethel's frying something that smells delicious." He looks at Martha and asks, "Where's Gordon?"

"He's not back from fishing yet. If you want something raw to take with you, one of us will get it for you," the slimmer lady says and gestures toward the case in the rear.

"No, we've come to eat here," Bob answers. He turns toward Rizzie and me. "You ladies grab us a table before they're all gone."

His advice is just in time because no sooner than we sit down, two more fishermen come in. One of the men takes a place at the last empty table. The other hands the rounder lady a stringer of fish and says, "How about fry up half of these for me and Sam. Put the rest on ice until we leave."

"Certainly," she answers him before turning back to Bob Everett and asking, "Bob, do you know what you want?"

He grins and says, "I know what we want, but I don't know if you have it today. Can you do three lobster rolls with sides of shaved fries?"

Martha laughs. "You're in luck. I made lobster salad first thing this morning."

South Carolina's coast offers all kinds of fish, and we get fine crabs, mussels, clams, and even frog legs here, but our waters aren't cold enough to catch lobsters. Restaurants that serve fresh lobster have tanks to keep them alive after they're shipped from up North. For the first time, I notice a large tank at the back of the kitchen with water bubbling all around live lobsters. I missed the skull and poppies when we entered the Skull Creek Goth Shop, and now I didn't notice the lobster tank. I must be slipping.

I've seen and heard "lobster rolls," but even though I grew up on the coast, I've never eaten one. I actually have this vague idea that Bob has ordered something similar to eggrolls offered in Chinese restaurants.

Ethel delivers four heaping platters of fried fish, potatoes, and hush puppies to the men who were already seated when we came in. In only a few minutes, she's at our table with three plates.

My first thought is, *She's made a mistake. Those are Po Boys,* because each plate has a sub roll on it beside a pickle spear and what my favorite deli when I was in college called "raw fries." They're the thinnest sliced fried potatoes I've ever seen.

I'm glad I don't comment that the order is wrong because Rizzie and Bob pick up half of their rolls and take big bites. That's when I see pink lobster flesh hanging from the rolls. I use my fork to open the sandwich. It's filled with what must be lobster salad—bites of lobster meat with specks of green and tiny minced celery barely held together with minimum mayo. One bite and I think I've died and gone to heaven. I've had warm, creamy Lobster Thermidor and eaten whole lobster at fancy restaurants when I lived in Columbia, South Carolina, but nothing touched this.

"Do you like it?" Bob Everett asks.

"I love it." I take another bite. "How about you, Rizzie?"

"It's one of the best things I've ever tasted, and I've been experimenting to make it just like this since the first time Bob brought me here."

So Rizzie has eaten here with Bob before. Her insistence on my coming with them wasn't her not wanting to be alone with him after all.

Friday, October 30

Chapter Fifteen

"OH," WAYNE SAYS, "You can tell your friend Bob Everett that the skull you and Ty found at the Halsey house is a model made of some fancy material similar to polyresin. There was even an extremely small model number stamped inside the lower jaw. It's embarrassing that I sent it to Columbia to be examined."

"So you've had the tape removed from the house?" I ask.

"Yes, but I don't want you or any of the kids going over there. The place isn't safe. Besides, the weather forecast is bad today."

I ask, "Do you think the weather will keep folks in this evening? Mike is so excited about playing in the band at Drew's."

"The day before Halloween? The bars will all be full tonight." He cuts me a stern look. "Don't forget. The Halsey house probably isn't a crime scene, but it's definitely not safe. I've taken the yellow tape down, but I don't want you there."

No response from me because that's exactly what I plan to do: go back to the Halsey place and look around. Only my respect for the law and its yellow tape kept me from prowling around there before. Since I saw the skull and crepe paper poppies at the Goth Shop, I've had this urge to thoroughly investigate that building. The fact the skull isn't legitimate might make it of no interest to Bob Everett and the sheriff, but not to me.

When Wayne leaves, I decide there's no time like the present. I'll ride over to the Halsey place and check out the rest of the house. Take a look in every room and closet to see if there are other signs that strange, weird events take place there. I realize I could have asked Wayne if they inspected every nook and cranny, but I know him too well. Showing so much interest would make him question my plans.

I dress in jeans and a sweatshirt, perfect attire to go rummaging through an old deserted house, but when I step outside, I find the television weatherman is right. The air has turned much colder than yesterday and last night. I return to my room and put on gray wool slacks, a gray and blue pullover sweater, a jacket, and a knitted stocking cap. I'm glad the coat isn't gray. I'd think I'd become the Gray Lady.

By the time I arrive at the long driveway up to

the Halsey house, I'm beginning to rethink my intentions. If someone has been practicing voodoo or root doctoring here, do I really want to risk sticking my nose into that business? The moss-laden oak trees that line the drive creating an arch that is beautiful in spring seems spooky now. The sun slips behind a cloud, leaving the trees and dirt drive draped in dull gray—perfect for the Gray Lady, but not for me.

An old Chevy pickup is pulled up beside the house. The truck looks so raggedy that I decide it must be abandoned. Was it there last Saturday? I don't know. I don't remember seeing it, but with all those teenagers there, I can't be sure.

Occasionally, I talk to myself. Okay, more often than I want to admit. *Callie, don't be childish. All you need to do is look around and see if there's evidence of anything else going on inside. You don't have to go near the barn where you were held captive way back when nor in the back woods where Bill wrecked the Mustang.*

I can't help but wonder if the Halsey place has some kind of hex on it—a spell that brings bad luck, especially for me and my family. Then I rationalize. When my brother Bill wrecked my car against that tree, he could have died, but he didn't. When that killer locked me in a stolen casket in the barn, I could have suffocated before the sheriff located me, but I survived.

I look down and see that the dirt at the foot of

the front steps is full of footprints. *Deputies, I think, Wayne's people who checked out the house or even still there from the students last Saturday.*

Then I realize that doesn't make sense. The recent rain would have washed out the footprints from last weekend. As I step up to the door, the thought occurs to me that the house may be locked. I reach out for the knob, half expecting to be greeted by some ghoul, but my fears aren't realized. The door doesn't swing open with some macabre creature waiting for me. The lock is old, so old that it's easily picked. (I will not divulge which of my brothers taught me to pick locks after Daddy developed the habit of locking us out if we weren't home by curfew time.)

Reading mystery books has taught me a lot. One of those lessons is to be aware of all senses— sight, hearing, touch, smell, and taste—in my surroundings. I have no intention of tasting anything I find, but I do want to pay close attention to my other senses. The two most prominent right now are smell and sight, though black clouds have arrived making it way too dark inside—shadowy—even though there are no curtains at the bare windows. My conspicuous smell awareness is the odor of candles—not the sweet scent of mixed berry that I like, nor the kitchen-like apple/cinnamon fragrance Jane prefers. This is the smoky odor left after something burns. Or maybe I'm wrong. There's a faint medicinal or herbal fragrance.

The open door to the living room on the right of the hall leads to a spacious area with a fireplace built into the outside wall. Across the mantel are burned-out candles in puddles of wax on saucers. A few feet from the opening lies a square piece of plywood. I've been in enough old houses to guess that it was used to block off the chimney, which is now open with charred wood and ashes that give a whiff of fairly fresh smoke. Someone has definitely been hanging out in here.

For a moment sunbeams shine through the windows—so bright I can see wisps of dust in them. Then the brightness disappears into darkness, and thunder rumbles—not in the distance, but nearby. I look out through the cracked glass of the windowpane as torrents of rain splatter the ground.

This is ridiculous, I think. *Somebody has been here, somebody had a fire not too long ago. I shouldn't have come here alone. Better to get Wayne or one of my brothers to come with me.* I'm tempted to go on back to town, but then, that's some hard rain. Maybe the storm will blow over. I may as well look around.

I'm standing by the window, looking out to see if the rain is going to let up when I feel something touch my shoulder.

To say I almost scream is a lie. I howl like a banshee as I glance back. Long, wrinkled black fingers rest on my shoulder. The hand belongs to a gloved figure wearing a hooded, black robe. It

200

takes a few minutes for me to recognize the face—
Raven or as his parents named him—Zachary
Blevins.

"What are you doing here?" I gasp.

"What are *you* doing here?" he asks.

"I came to look through the house, to see if
there's any other evidence that people were trying
to work root here," I say.

"What makes you think that?" Zack moves his
hand.

"I went to Skull Creek Goth Shop where I saw
exactly the same setup that Ty and I fell into. The
lady there said it's supposed to enable dreamers
to have contact with the deceased."

"That's exactly what she told me. Now I've
come to see if it's true." His face crumples. "I've
got to talk to my dad. I have to know if he took
his life because of me."

"What makes you think that?"

Zack brushes his hand down the black robe.
"Because he hated this. We had an argument the
day before he died. He thought my dark ways
were ridiculous, said I embarrassed him with my
silliness. Told me I was a disappointment to him."

"Probably words said in anger," I try to
comfort.

The boy bursts into tears that quickly turn to
sobs.

"I have to know. I've got a sleeping bag in the
car. I plan to spend the night here and see if
he'll come to me and tell me if I caused him to

do what he did."

"What about the skull and poppies? A deputy took those away."

"I have more in the car. I bought them at the Goth Shop. I put the ones you and Ty found beneath the stairs. I planned to be the one who discovered them. Then I would have put skulls around town to stir up some mystery and PR for the TEAM haunted house. I didn't intend for anyone to get hurt." He shrugs his shoulders. "I bought the skulls and poppies to promote the haunted house. They caused the house to be changed to a haunted graveyard. Now, it's been called off, too. The whole Fall Festival has been cancelled. I'm going to use the skulls and those flowers to reach my father."

"I'm fine, so don't worry about my being hurt. The woman at the shop said that the skull and poppies can be used to call up spirits. Is that what you plan to do?"

"She told me, too, but at first I just wanted to do something to get people talking about a skull being found where the haunted house would be. I didn't realize that it would keep us from using the Halsey place. Now I want to use the skull and poppies to help Dad come through to me."

His face lights up. "Will you stay? I'll let you use the sleeping bag, and I have a whole lot of bottled water and snacks."

"I have to go to work." I almost tell him that I have to be at the funeral home when his mother comes to make funeral arrangements for his father, but then I decide that's not a good idea.

"Will you come back tonight when you get off work? Maybe Dad's spirit will contact me even quicker if you're here since you're who found his body."

"What about your mom? Won't she expect you to be home tonight? She doesn't need to be worried about where you are."

"She's so upset that she won't know if I'm there or not." His eyes glisten with tears. "Will you stay with me?"

"I can't do that, Zack," I say, thinking, *That's the last thing I need to do—spend the night with a teenager. I'm not a teacher anymore, but not an idiot either. These days and times, no telling what I'd be accused of.*

"Please think about it." Zack looks around, and then adds, "I'm going out to get my things." He's barely out the door before the rain intensifies, its sound echoing through the room as it beats on the roof.

Zack comes back in with water drenching his face and dripping from his body. The rolled-up sleeping bag and large backpack he carries are soaking wet. He throws them both to the floor, and his hood flips back, I see that Zack's head is shaved completely bald.

I can't help gasping, "What happened to your hair?"

"My father hated my long hair. I cut it and

then shaved my head after the sheriff came and told us Dad was dead."

The rumble of thunder and flashing of lightning come closer and closer together. I want nothing more than to leave—to get away from this house and this boy. I know he's in psychological pain and I should help him in some way, but I have no idea how.

I sit down on the floor to wait out the storm. Zack kneels and begins unloading food and drinks from his backpack.

The bounce comes at the same time I hear a humongous clap of thunder. My behind feels the way my shoulder does from the recoil when I fire a shotgun. It's like the old wooden floor has kicked me in the tush.

Zack falls over the sleeping bag. He shouts, "What happened?"

I look up at the corner of the outside wall of the room. Flames lick across the ceiling.

"Get out!" I yell. "The house is on fire."

Zack and I reach the front stoop together. We run through the pounding rain which doesn't stop the fire. He jumps in the Chevy truck, and I slide into the Corvette. We rev both engines and drive down the driveway, him right behind me. When we stop, I look back as the house goes up like kindling. Zack gets out and walks through the pouring rain to the passenger side of my car. He opens the door and asks, "What happened?"

"Lightning struck," I reply.

"Did you call 911?" he asks.

"No, I didn't, and I'm not thinking you should either," I answer. "Let it burn."

A MUTED INSTRUMENTAL VERSION of "I Saw the Light" summons me to the funeral home's door. Expecting to greet Sammy Bee's widow, Mrs. Blevins, I'm surprised to see a child, a little girl. Then I realize that she is a small full-grown woman. She's not quite five feet tall and can't weigh as much as ninety pounds.

The lady extends her hand and says, "Hello, I'm Joan Blevins. I have an appointment to discuss funeral arrangements for my husband Sam Blevins."

"Yes, ma'am," I reply, "Mr. Otis Middleton and I will be assisting you. Come with me." I lead her to the Rose Room and buzz Otis that Mrs. Blevins has arrived.

As I begin to close the door behind us, Mrs. Blevins asks, "Can you leave that open? My daughter is parking the car and will need to see where we are."

"No problem," I answer as Otis comes in and "The Old Rugged Cross" announces that the front door is open again. A tall, thin woman joins us.

Mrs. Blevins introduces her daughter Jean and then continues, "I know that some people, including my daughter here, think a funeral following a person taking his own life should be subdued, but I disagree."

Otis assures that Middleton's always strives to provide exactly the services the family desires.

"Sammy was my high school sweetheart," Mrs. Blevins says. "I don't know what caused him to end his own life this way. We had no marital or financial problems, and to my knowledge, he hadn't been diagnosed with some dreadful disease. What I do know is that one horrible day out of a lifetime as a good husband, father, and citizen shouldn't be the way he's remembered." She removes a handkerchief from her handbag and dabs at her eyes.

The daughter puts her arm around her mother's shoulder and says, "Mama, why don't we wait until Julia gets home and Zack is feeling better to make decisions. You may see things differently after a few days."

The mother looks at her daughter with fire in her eyes. "I'm not seeing anything other than how I want it. I told you when you insisted on driving me here that as his wife, I will make the decisions, not you kids."

Otis cuts me a glance that says, "Oh, no, this one's gonna be tough."

"First," Mrs. Blevins says, turning away from her daughter and toward Otis, "I want this to truly be a celebration of Sam's life. I want it to be a party, and I want champagne toasts after a couple of eulogies given by members of his family and his friends."

She pauses and then collapses in tears. Jean embraces her mother. "It's okay, Mama," she says. "We'll do it your way."

"I know we will," Mrs. Blevins says. "I was just thinking that two of his friends who would have been happy to speak for him are dead. I can't believe that both Melvin and Norm died this week." She pauses. "Could that be why Sam did what he did?" She looks up into Jean's face. "He was so upset when he came home from Melvin's service. He said he's buried dogs with more honor than that." She glares at Otis.

Knowing Otis as well as I do, I catch the slight bristling in his manner, but it doesn't seem obvious to anyone else. "Those were Mrs. Barnes's wishes," Otis says. "As I said, we always try to fulfill the family's requests. We will supply whatever you want however you want it, just as we followed Mrs. Barnes's instructions."

"She wants a casket shaped like a car . . . " Janet blurts in an aggravated tone.

"Yes, I do," Mrs. Blevins interrupts. "Next to his family, Sam loved automobiles as much as anything on earth. I've seen custom coffins in those newspapers I buy at the supermarket, and I want one for Sam."

"I'm certain we can supply whatever you want," Otis assures her.

Jean grimaces and says, "She's talking about those weekly yellow journalism papers like *The Inquiry*. She's addicted to those things."

"I am not," Mrs. Blevins protests.

"Do they really make caskets shaped like cars?" Jean asks Otis.

"Yes, ma'am," Otis answers. "Callie, would you get a catalog of customs and bring it for Mrs. Blevins to see?"

When I return with the book, it doesn't take Mrs. Blevins long to select a custom-made casket shaped and decorated like a sports car. "Can you get this one?" she asks.

"Yes," Otis answers, "but of course we don't have that in stock. We'll have to see how long it will take for delivery before you set the date for the visitation and service."

"Oh, I already know that. My oldest child is out of the country. We'll need to know when she'll be back and whether the cousins in California will be coming before we can schedule anything. I just want to plan everything and have you order what we'll need."

Her spirits seem to lift as she adds, "I'm thinking about having Sam lie in state in the showroom at the car lot."

Jean's face screws into a grimace, but she doesn't say anything.

Otis keeps writing on the paper on his clipboard. "Will we be serving refreshments for the visitation or the 'lying in state'?" he asks.

"I'll have to think about that. I know I want the champagne toasts, but in the past, Sam quit serving much in the way of food at the store because people got it into the display cars."

"Mother," Jean says, "I'm sure that Mr. Middleton can supply us with a large space for a wake or visitation.   You don't want Father's services to turn into a circus."

Mrs. Blevins stands.   "Maybe it will be better if we firm up the plans after I know when we can have the services." She turns toward Jean and says, "Will you bring the car around to the steps?"

Otis is squirming. "We'll need your signature authorizing body prep, and I can't order the special unit without a deposit and you sign for it."

"Just show me where to put my John Henry," Mrs. Blevins says as she waves Jean toward the door.

When Jean is gone and the papers are signed, Mrs. Blevins whispers, "I'll come back without her."

Chapter Sixteen

BY THE TIME I GET AWAY from work, there's no time to create a unique costume for the contest at Drew's Tavern tonight, so I'm taking the easy way out. I stop at Party Palace and buy a pair of cat ears on a head band and a clip-on black tail. I have black leggings and black boots already.

Standing in front of the mirror on the back of my bedroom door, I'm a bit disappointed. My legs look good in the leggings, but then people have always told me I have great legs. I don't look voluptuous though. Ever since I started hiding my flatness with inflatable bras and padded panties, I've maintained a feminine but modest shape. What rocks it in regular clothes leaves me lackluster in a black T-shirt even with the sassy tail clipped on.

Only one thing to do. I strip down, lay my bra

on the table, and get the little pump out of the closet. It only takes a few minutes to go from A+ or maybe B to C (or perhaps even D). I use a ruler to be sure that both sides rise in equal splendor before putting my underwear and clothing back on. With my hair tousled all around and the ears on, I step up to the mirror and give myself a long, seductive *meow* before doing a full smoky eye makeup. I'm drawing on whiskers with eyebrow pencil when my cell phone sounds.

"What are you doing?" Wayne asks.

"Finishing up my costume for tonight. I wish you could come out to Drew's for the contest."

"I'm tied up with an investigation. You have fun with your friends and tell Mike I hate I can't be there."

"Will do," I reply as I finish the whiskers.

"What are you wearing?" he asks.

"Just a cat costume. Not a chance of my winning. I bought a tail and ears, but other than that, I have on black leggings and tee with my black boots."

"The thigh-high boots?" he asks.

"Yes," I answer, and he bursts into laughter.

"Put on a hat with a feather and tell them you came as Puss in Boots," he laughs and then quickly adds, "Excuse me. I couldn't resist that," as though I might be offended.

I laugh out loud right back at him before disconnecting and going over to Jane's door. When I knock, I'm met by Medusa. I've seen her in this costume before. I don't know why that particular Greek myth of the human female with living serpents for hair fascinates her so, but it has since we studied Medusa in high school. She bought the costume a few years later and wears it every Halloween whether she's going out or stays home passing out treats. She hands me a miniature Snickers bar as soon as we're seated in the car.

"Here's your treat," she says. "I bought a bag of them expecting trick or treaters might come by before we left for Drew's."

I take a bite and hope she bought a big bag. Snickers—my favorite candy bar.

"How did you manage to get away for our girls' night out?" I ask. "I was afraid you had a date with Frankie."

"He drove Mike to the club at eight o'clock. The band has to be there early even though they don't start playing until ten. He said for us to come and wait in the parking lot to see Drew arrive at nine."

"Well, we should get there just before nine. Rizzie and Allie are meeting us at Drew's and want us all to go in together."

"How are you dressed?" Jane asks.

"Cat Woman, but Wayne says I'm Puss in Boots since I'm wearing my thigh-high boots."

Jane giggles and then asks, "Which one?"

"What do you mean?"

"Lots of actresses have played the part of Cat

212

Woman. Which one are you most like?"

I laugh. "Going back to the old days. Makeup like Julie Newmar, but I'm gonna purr like Eartha Kitt."

THE FACT NO ONE HAS FALLEN down the steps at Drew's Tavern is a miracle. The club is built on a hill with the parking area near the bottom. To reach the door, customers have to climb a narrow flight of steps up to the door. Metal pipe serves as handrails on both sides as well as discouraging new arrivals from breaking in line when the steps are crowded with people coming from the parking lot or street.

I'm relieved to find that someone—probably Mike—has put orange cones with a sign that reads "Reserved for Callie" in the space closest to the steps. "DREW'S PLACE" is painted on a sign at the front of the spot. I've heard that Drew is as persnickety about that parking place as Sheldon is about his seat on the couch in *The Big Bang Theory.* I wonder where Drew's going to park tonight.

The Vette is barely stopped when Rizzie and Allie approach. I can't believe Allie's costume. She's apparently Little Red Riding Hood because what's she's done is add a hooded red cape to her red dress from the reunion. Same ta-tas bursting out of the neckline and same red stiletto heels. I'm glad I pumped my chest up.

Rizzie takes an even easier route than mine since what she's wearing is not a completely unusual way for her to dress. A Gullah lady, she's wearing authentic African cloth wrapped around her body, a smaller piece around her head, and tons of handmade jewelry. "Are we ready to go in?" she asks.

"Mike said to wait and watch Drew arrive at nine o'clock. He wouldn't tell me why but told me it's worth seeing," I reply.

Allie motions toward the rear of the lot toward the streetlights. "Do you ladies want to move back to my car where there's more seating?" Allie asks.

There's now a line of people moving up the steps one by one as the doorman cards customers at the door.

"Let's just sit on the hood of the car," Jane suggests.

"Not no, but hell no!" I exclaim, forgetting all about kindergarten cussing. "Not that any of us have Kardashian behinds, but I'm not risking a bucket butt putting a dent in the hood of this car."

"Why don't we sit on the stairway?" Jane asks.

"Because there's a line of people on the steps," Rizzie answers.

We're saved from this dilemma by Drew's arrival. A white stretch limousine pulls up on the road beside the steps. It stops, and a uniformed driver wearing a chauffeur's cap exits and walks back. He opens a door for the passenger.

Out steps Elvis in all the full-fledged splendor everyone has seen on television and YouTube—the Las Vegas video—wearing a bell-bottomed white jumpsuit bedazzled in silver. The stand-up collar and bare chest are pure Elvis. The only thing different is that Drew isn't wearing a wig, nor has he dyed his prematurely gray hair. If Elvis had only known how good he would look with lighter hair, he could have saved a lot of money by abandoning the black hair dye. I wonder why the limo didn't park where the passenger door would be at the foot of the stairs, and I soon see why. In a macho move, Drew lifts his leg and steps over the pipe railing between the small landing at the entrance and the road, putting him directly in front of the door which the doorman swings open with a flourish.

"Well," I say when the door closes behind him and I hear the crowd erupt in applause, "we've seen the arrival. Let's go in and see the show."

Except for the bandstand, the inside of the club is almost as dark as the night is outside. It's crowded and noisy with voices as well as the DJ music, which happens to be "The Monster Mash" as we enter, and Drew stands on the bandstand surrounded by monsters.

The drummer is a purple people eater. I always wondered if "purple" referred to the alien or the people he ate. The drummer interprets the word to mean both. He wears purple clothes with attached purple wings. A partial face mask supplies the impression that he has one eye in the middle of his forehead right above a big purple horn coming from his nose area. Attached to the sleeves are dolls with faces painted purple.

If I didn't know Mike is playing bass for this gig, I would not recognize the tall green creature as my brother. He's covered with green scaly-looking cloth, including over his gigantic three-toed feet. The hood covers his head completely and features a mouth that makes me think of a large-mouthed bass filled with shark-type teeth. Red cellophane covers Mike's eyes and extends in all directions creating the illusion of very big eyes. He's South Carolina's very own Lizard Man who has appeared up in Lee County and nearby off and on since the eighties.

The lead guitar player is absolutely the most hideous, gruesome zombie I ever saw, and with my brothers and since dating Wayne, I've seen too many zombie movies.

The place is packed, and I don't see any empty tables though there are a few seats left at the bar. None of them are side by side. I look around, hoping someone will leave.

A tall Bigfoot approaches us. This guy has to be six feet, three inches, or higher. He's covered with brown fur and has accented the name by wearing gigantic false feet. His feet, hands, and face are covered with dark brown makeup instead of fur. "Callie?" he asks.

I nod yes.

"I'm Rick, the bouncer. Mike reserved a table for you. He also said if anyone bothers any of you, let me know." He looks down at Allie's cleavage, and I can tell he's thinking she might get too much attention.

As we follow him to the table, I say, "Great costume. Bigfoot, right?"

"Another name for Bigfoot. The ones that have been sighted in the Carolinas are generally referred to as Carolina Woolyboogers, Boojums, or Skunk Apes." He pulls my chair out for me. "I've been on a few hunts for one in the upper part of the state. I got interested after I heard Randall Hylton's song, 'Bigfoot.' Have you ever heard it?"

I don't tell him that I saw the late, great singer/songwriter Randall Hylton himself perform that ridiculous song about being seduced by a female Bigfoot at Bill's Pickin' Parlor when I lived in Columbia. I also heard a Hylton impersonator who almost captured my heart sing it at a bluegrass festival. I keep my mouth shut and don't reply to this bouncer's lecture. Seems everyone I meet these days is determined to educate me.

A cute waitress in a Wonder Woman costume takes our orders—beer for everyone else but gingerale for me. I don't deny that I hit a few happy hours in my younger years, but since I grew up and began thinking like an adult, I don't drink and drive at all—not even a glass of wine or draft beer if I'm driving. Okay—so I don't want to risk an expensive ticket or a night in jail, but the real reason is that I've cosmetized a few victims of DUI accidents. Makes a body think, and I don't mean the body I'm working on.

From the time the band kicks off, my friends and I are dancing. Of course, it's hard to identify our partners because of the costumes. Allie is on the dance floor with one creature after another. It's obvious that she's enjoying herself, but she's not moving nearly so seductively as she did with Melvin Barnes at the reunion.

Drew's introduction of the band members ends with, "And now a song from our guest bass player tonight—Mike Parrish."

Ooo eee, ooo ah ah, ting tang, walla walla, bing bang, ooo eee, ooo ah ah, ting tang, walla walla bing bang, oo eee ah ah, ting tang, walla walla bing bang Mike sings out, and I'm expecting the next line to be, "I told the witch doctor I was in love with you," but instead Mike sings, "I told the root doctor I was in love with you."

This is such a surprise to Rizzie that she laughs so hard she spews beer across the table. I'm giggling at Rizzie when I notice Fletcher Williams. He's dancing without a partner, and he's got some good moves considering his level of intoxication is obviously extreme. He glances over at our table and stops moving. After a minute of standing still, his eyes dart around the room as if he's frantically searching for something or someone.

I can't believe it! Fletcher drops to his knees, crawls from the dance floor, and winds up crouched beneath a table where several women are seated. They obviously don't know Fletcher. Their expressions show shock as they stand up and back away. Bigfoot Rick rushes up and bends over. He says something to Fletch and then offers him a hand, helps him from the floor, and guides him away. Seems like someone is always leading Fletcher off the scene.

"What was that all about?" Rizzie asks.

"Poor old Fletcher Williams, drunk again," Allie responds.

"He was looking at us when he stopped dancing," I say. "He's really out of it. Maybe when he saw me, he figured the sheriff was with me and would arrest him for drinking too much."

"I hope he's not driving," Jane says.

"Wayne told me that's about Fletcher's only virtue," I tell her. "He doesn't ever drive a car. He either walks or rides his bicycle wherever he goes."

"That's good," Jane answers. "At least he won't be out on the road harming anyone."

"Could be dangerous for him though," Allie comments, and I know she's thinking about her sister Josie dying as a result of being hit while riding her bike.

During the band's first break, Rizzie points across the room to a tall woman wearing skin-tight black leather pants and a vest-type top that shows a lot of cleavage. Her high black boots are similar to mine but with taller heels. She has on a black half mask, but it doesn't hide her obvious beauty. Her dark hair falls in a braid almost to her waist. Daggers and knives adorn her.

"What kind of costume is that?" Rizzie asks.

"You obviously don't read urban fantasy," Allie says.

"As busy as the grill keeps me, I don't have time to read much of anything for pleasure," Rizzie answers.

"She's Jane Yellowrock, a vampire killer in a series by Faith Hunter," Allie tells her.

"I guess that accounts for the weapons and the fact that ever since I noticed her, she's turned down anyone who wasn't wearing a vampire costume when they asked her to dance."

"You're very observant," Jane comments.

The conversation goes into another direction when a tall, masked vampire approaches our table, leans over Jane, and whispers, "I'm going to bite your neck," in a hoarse voice.

Jane jumps as though she's been shot while the rest of us laugh. The vampire adds, "It's me, Frankie" in his normal tone.

He joins us, relieving me of having to wait until my friends are ready to go before I can leave. As much as I love music and my brothers, I'm tired. The thought of my warm bed appeals more than staying at Drew's Tavern to hear Mike and watch

Frankie flirt with my friend Jane.

When the intermission ends and the band begins playing again, the Jane Yellowrock woman comes over to our table and asks Frankie to dance. He politely declines, explaining, "Thanks, but I'm here with my girlfriend."

Jane Yellowrock explodes. "Moving mighty fast, aren't you? Our relationship isn't over yet and you've moved on!" She slaps Frankie across the face, pulls a knife from the scabbard on her hip, and draws it back, poised to strike. "When I get through with you, nobody will want you," she says.

Bigfoot Rick appears behind Yellowrock and pulls her away from Frankie. He wrestles the knife from her. The half mask slips and I see that Jane Yellowrock is Madison. Lizard Man Mike leaps off the stage mid-song and rushes over to our table screaming, "Madison, you're crazy! That's my brother Frank, not me!"

Restrained by the bouncer holding her arms behind her, Madison spits into Mike's face. "You were a vampire last year and as much as you like the Jane Yellowrock books, I thought you'd be a vampire when I heard you were playing with Drew's band tonight.."

"All irrelevant," Rick says. "You've assaulted someone here in the club. Our policy requires that I call law enforcement." He turns toward Frankie. "Do you want to press charges?"

"I don't guess so," Frankie says, though I can

tell that's exactly what he'd like to do.

"Then I'll just take this little wildcat back to the office and call the cops. I want a report made even if they don't take her to jail." He looks down into Madison's teary eyes. "And you're officially barred from coming back here."

At that point, Madison begins crying and begging for the incident to just be forgotten. "I promise I'll leave you alone," she tells Mike as he turns his back to her and returns to the stage.

With Frankie here to take care of my friend Jane, I excuse myself and go to my car.

I look down, and there on my shiny new bumper is a sticker that reads "I climbed the hill to DREW'S TAVERN." I bend over and try to peel it off, but it's stuck tight. I don't really want my car defaced with bar bumper stickers, and I certainly don't need a reminder of how close one of my brothers came to being stabbed tonight.

Saturday, October 31

Chapter Seventeen

ANOTHER DAY SPENT SEARCHING for Big Boy with no luck. I rarely feel sorry for myself because I'm really blessed. A wonderful family. A job doing work that makes me feel like I help ease the pain of those who have lost loved ones. A good man who loves me, and devoted friends.

So why am I having a pity party at twilight? I've spent the day alone. Jane is with Frankie, and Rizzie went to some "dig" with Bob Everett. Their being with male friends would be fine except that I have the day off from work, and *my* man is working.

I admit, I whined, "Why?" this morning when Wayne told me he'd be gone all day.

"Callie," he answered, "Good old fashioned police work is as important as modern forensics to crime detection. I'll be doing some of both."

"I was hoping we could go somewhere, do something together, and look for Big Boy."

"Actually, what I'm working on may help find him," Wayne said.

"I'm about ready to give up on my dog."

"Remember this, Callie, an important factor in law enforcement is that criminals aren't required to pass an intelligence test. Plain old stupidity leads to lots of arrests. My job is to seek out criminals, including those I think stole your dog. Sooner or later, they'll make a stupid mistake, and we'll catch them."

I guess that was supposed to appease me about how little time he has for me sometimes, but it didn't.

After Wayne left, I set out driving around, still looking and calling for Big Boy.

To make matters worse, the white Econoline that reminds me of the one with "Animal Rescue" on it seems to be everywhere I go. If it weren't so ridiculous, I'd think the men in it were following me. I'm not scared. I just don't like it.

When Tina Turner sings out of my telephone, I hope it's Wayne to tell me he managed to get off after all and we can have dinner together.

"Hey, honey," I answer.

"This isn't honey, it's Allie," I hear.

"Sorry. I thought you were Wayne."

"I've kind of got my place set up, and I'd like for you to come see it," she says. "Besides, I want to talk with you."

There's no reason not to go. Nothing better to do. Allie gives me directions to her place at Hidden Lake, and I head that way after keying in the location on my phone GPS just to be on the safe side.

Thunk! Something as big as that Ford Econoline hitting the back of my Corvette should make a loud crash, but the sound doesn't boom. I would also expect a bone-jarring collision, but I'm barely thrown forward against my seat belt as the phone flies from my hand.

If the impact were harder, I'd feel pain, maybe even apprehension, but I'm overwhelmed with guttural anger. How dare that fool hit my Vette? Has he dented it? The click as I unfasten my seat belt is simultaneous with my flinging the car door open and leaping out.

My brothers are big guys, each about six feet tall, but they'd look small beside the man standing at the back of my car. I'd estimate at least six feet, five, maybe as much as two inches taller, and BIG. I don't mean fat; I mean wide, hefty, and muscle-bound. He's wearing all black—pants, T-shirt, and a hoodie with black combat boots. Immediately I think of him with the name of a Stephen King character—Big Driver.

"Why'd you slam on brakes?" Driver demands in a low voice, but I get the feeling the question is irrelevant. Did he rear-end me on purpose?

"What do you mean?" I snap back and point to the stop sign. "Are you blind or can't you read?

What did you expect me to do at the intersection?"

I lean over and examine the front bumper of the Econoline wedged against the back of the Vette. The huge man stands slightly behind me, his attention fixed on the scratch and dent his van put in my Corvette. If my car weren't so new, I'd be inclined to let it go since the damage is small, but this first mark on my yellow baby infuriates me.

"You're going to pay for this." Spittle flies out with my words.

"Let me get a tool and be sure we can disengage the vehicles without causing further damage," Driver says and opens the back of the Econoline. The inside is dark.

Another man, also dressed in all black, suddenly appears in the opening and jumps out beside Driver.

"If you'd drop looking for your big old dog, this wouldn't be necessary," the second man says to me in a hateful tone.

"Don't waste your time talking to her, Obee. Let's put her in the van and get out of here. You drive her car."

"I don't want you telling me what to do, but I won't argue about driving that Corvette. I've wanted to get behind the steering wheel of that beauty since the first time she tried to stop us."

"Then shut your pie hole, and let's get going."

For once in my life, I'm speechless. Obee grabs me from behind, pins my arms against my sides, and lifts me off the ground. I open my mouth to scream, but Driver slaps a piece of tape across my mouth. I arch my back trying to free myself, but the massive arms around me grip even tighter. There is nothing I can do as I'm lifted and thrown into the back of the Econoline.

I can't catch my breath, and the sour taste of regurgitated Quarter Pounder I picked up for lunch rises in my throat in a blinding explosion of nausea. Terrified I'll choke to death, I swallow it back down.

The rear doors of the Econoline slam so hard that I feel a *whoosh* of air as they close. The bang is louder than the noise I heard when the van hit my car. Then the ignition sounds and I feel the vehicle moving. I lie there with my head down, face against the ribbed metal floor, helpless and hopeless.

My next sensation is of being touched. Not anything uncomfortable—a gentle nuzzling. My eyes adjust to the dimness and I look into the face of an animal, a large, brown dog with dark, soulful eyes. My first impulse is to pull away in fear of being bitten, but that's not happening. The dog's jaws are taped together with gray duct tape, but I can still identify its doggy face's breed as boxer. It backs away when I lift my head higher. I focus behind the animal and see another boxer—a brindle. Beside it is a smaller dog. I can't identify the breed—probably a mix of some kind. These two also have their jaws bound shut with duct tape.

After what seems like eternity, the vehicle stops. Someone opens the back and Driver grabs my ankles and drags me to the door. Obee stands watching with a big grin on his face and says, "Come on out, nosy. We've got to put you in storage until we decide what to do with you. Don't have time for any prying women right now."

Driver stands me on the gravel roadway, but my legs are too weak and shaky to support me. I crumple. They pick me up with Driver holding both ankles and Obee gripping my wrists so hard they hurt. The two men carry me into a metal prefab building similar to the casket warehouse behind Middleton's, except that the coffins are lined up neatly while the containers in this building are scattered helter-skelter.

The place is badly lit and stinks, but the eerie silence bothers me most. About a dozen boxes made of metal bars are crowded into the room, but there's no order to them. They appear to be shoved in all directions. I realize they're animal crates of several sizes filled with dogs—two or more animals crammed into some of them.

The expectation from so many dogs is loud barking, but the only sounds are soft thumps as a few of them lunge against the bars while others lie motionless as though they've given up all hope of escape. Or of food or water as I see no bowls in or out of the crates. The caged animals vary in size, color, and breed, but they all share two characteristics. Their mouths are bound shut with gray tape, and their eyes are sad, more than sad—sorrowful.

"Put her in the large crate in back." I can't tell who's talking—Driver or Obee, but I assume it's Driver since he seems to be the boss. Loud, raucous laughter from both of them.

"The one beside the black and white spotted Great Dane? I think that's the dog she's been looking for." They giggle like low-throated school girls.

One of the men grips my arm and force-walks me beside him with his forward movement. I attempt to flail and struggle, but the man kicks my feet out from under me. I go down on my back, flinging my arms across my face to ward off the vicious kick I see coming at me. I'm lifted, carried to an open crate. They throw me inside. My feet stick out, and Driver brutally bends my legs and forces them into the crate. Metal clanks as he slams the door shut. Both men giggle again when Driver adds a padlock to the latch on the closure.

Big Boy is in the crate beside me. I've found my dog. I've said it before and I repeat it now. My dog smiles. If his mouth weren't taped, he'd grin now. His eyes light up and he nudges himself against the side of the crate adjacent to mine. At his feet, a matted black and white dog so shaggy I can barely see its eyes cowers no more than ten inches tall at the shoulder and probably fewer than twelve pounds as it pushes against Big Boy's front legs.

Panic-stricken and horrified, I don't even feel relief at seeing Big Boy. Crouched on hands and knees, I can think of nothing that might help us. I believe I will go stark, raving mad.

"WHAT THE (f-word) DID YOU THINK YOU WERE DOING? OR DID YOU IDIOTS THINK AT ALL?"

The voice booms. Bounces against the walls. I look across the crates toward the now-open bay doors of the building. Driver and Obee walk toward me beside a much slimmer, shorter man with dark hair. He isn't dressed in black. His slacks are dark chocolate, and the sweater vest he wears over a long-sleeved, cream-colored shirt, is patterned with triangular shades of coffee. Instead of boots, he has on expensive-looking loafers. The deafening words come from him.

"Get her out of there," he commands as they reach me. "Tell me again why you have her, why you brought her here."

Driver takes a key from his pocket and opens the padlock. He reaches in and drags me out. My limbs are asleep and I fall to the floor. No one touches me. I lie in total shock, trying to regain sensation in my arms and legs while they talk.

"She stopped us," Driver says, "and asked us about her dog. We kept seeing her all over. We got worried she was onto us."

"And . . ."

"And we liked her car," Obee adds. "Figured we could get a lot of money for the parts."

"So why is her car sitting in the yard instead of at the chop shop?"

"We decided you might want to get it painted and keep it for yourself."

The smaller man snorts and says, "What about the woman? What plans do you have for her?"

Driver laughs. I look up at him. His face is demonical. "Obee and I want to make her a snuff film queen—a very special snuff film."

Scrambling to try to get up, I'm so shocked by his words that I fall to my knees again. A snuff film? I know what that means—a film of someone dying.

"Tell me about it." The smaller man's tone is mocking.

"We plan to put her in the ring with Killer."

"Do you realize the jail time we'd get for dog-fighting is nothing next to murder, especially for letting a fight dog kill a woman?"

"Only if we get caught, Ace."

"I've told you before. Call me Andy or Mr. Evans, not Ace."

"Yes, sir, but we're all in this together even if you don't want to get your hands dirty."

"I'm not having anything to do with a snuff film, and you're both fools. Do you know who this woman is?"

"She's the one who's been harassing us about

her dog."

"Do we have her dog?"

"It's the black and white Great Dane bait dog."

"Get it. She's the local sheriff's girlfriend. We have to get rid of her and the dog." He reaches out and offers me his hand as I try to stand, but as soon as I'm on my feet, he whips out an orange plastic zip-tie from his pocket and cuffs my wrists together with it. He pushes me toward the door.

Obee follows with Big Boy on a leash. The choke collar is so tight that flesh and fur bulge out around it, but the dog still reacts to the sight of me by trying to break away and reach me.

"Her dog?" Andy asks.

"Yep," Driver says.

"What are we gonna do with them, Ace?" asks Obee.

"Put them both in the back of the van for now." Andy smiles at me. "But first, hose out the floor. I've told you to keep things cleaner than you do. It smells bad enough without you letting dog poop lie around. There's some on the floor in the buildings, too." He chuckles and adds, "What we aren't going to do is take either of them anywhere near tonight's fight."

I'm hoping that Andy has kinder plans for me or that I can do something—anything to save Big Boy and me, but no. Nada. Zero. Nil. Naught. Absolutely nothing I can do to help myself or my dog, and I don't know what to expect from the neat, clean Mr. Evans. After Wayne's lecture on being prepared, where is the stun gun he gave me? In my jacket pocket on the front seat of my Vette. Where is my pepper spray? In the dash pocket of the car like it will do me any good there. Where's my fancy phone? I don't even know.

Big Boy's jaws are taped shut but he growls deep in his throat as Obee pulls him toward the door. Though not on a leash, the little black and white dog comes with them, right by Big Boy's side. Andy kicks the backs of my legs to speed me up walking in the same direction.

Suddenly, powerful lights flood the darkness, and amplified words blare into the night: "PUT YOUR HANDS ON YOUR HEAD AND HIT THE GROUND."

The sound and brightness surround us. Driver and Obee drop facedown with no resistance. Obee still clutches the dog leash.

I've never before felt what happens next, but I know immediately what it is. Andy presses a gun barrel against the side of my head, right over my left temple. He looks frantically around at the other metal building, the Econoline, my Vette, and a silver Jaguar surrounded by police vehicles with red and blue lights throbbing.

"Don't think I won't shoot her," Andy yells.

"PUT THE GUN DOWN."

I recognize the sheriff's voice through the electronic magnification.

"No. I'll kill her unless you help me get away."

"PUT THE GUN DOWN. I WON'T NEGOTIATE

WITH YOU."

"If you don't meet my demands, she'll die."

"I WON'T NEGOTIATE WITH YOU. RIGHT NOW YOUR CHARGES ARE ALL RELATED TO THE DOG FIGHTS. DON'T MAKE IT MURDER."

"You're not very concerned about your girlfriend."

"PUT THE GUN DOWN."

My heart heaves in my chest, pounding against my rib cage at what feels like a hundred miles a minute. Will Wayne let the man shoot me? Sometimes I wonder whether my love for him is big enough for long-term commitment and marriage, but I never before doubted his love for me.

I swear I actually *hear* the chain hit the ground when Obee lets go of the leash holding Big Boy.

The next sound is a gunshot and scream as a body thumps to the ground. I realize that I am now lying down. Was that thud me? Have I been shot? I don't hurt anywhere. A heavy warmth presses against me. Is it blood? It only takes a moment to realize what I feel is the weight of Big Boy against me. I gag at the thought Andy shot my dog. Law enforcement officers rush up, but they're busy cuffing Andy and moving him away. The sheriff wraps his arms around me and says, "This will hurt." He yanks the tape from my mouth—fast like Daddy did when he had to remove a bandage when I was a little girl. We're both shaking.

"Did you shoot Andy?" I ask.

"Big Boy charged him to get to you when the big man let go of the chain. Knocked him over and his gun went off."

"So you would have let him shoot me?"

"Callie, this place is surrounded and on top of that other building is the best SWAT sniper available." Wayne pulls back a bit. "Can't believe it. You're crying."

"Of course, I'm crying. I was scared to death."

"But you throw up when you're scared."

"Glad I didn't with that tape on my mouth." I tremble. "How did you find me?"

"Your phone GPS was on. When you never showed up to meet Alice and didn't answer her calls, she started blowing up my phone about you. Multiple law enforcement agencies have been working on the dog-fighting ring for months. I didn't expect you to get mixed up in it in any way until Big Boy was snatched to use as a bait dog. Even then, I had no idea they'd grab you, too."

A paramedic runs up to us. "Sheriff, please let her go. I need to check her out."

"I'm fine," I say, look down, and then add, "except for a couple of scrapes on my knees."

"Let me take a look." Without another word, he uses scissors to split the sides of my pants.

Wayne releases me from his arms and begins issuing instructions to the deputies and others. The EMT cleans the skinned places on my knees and the palms of my hands before announcing that I'm released and can leave whenever I'm ready. I head toward my Corvette, but a deputy stops me.

"I'm sorry, Ms. Parrish, but we have to impound your car so forensics can check it out for fingerprints. One of them drove it, didn't he?"

I nod yes.

"Someone will give you a ride home, and we'll take your dogs to the vet to have the tape around their mouths removed," he continues.

"I only have one dog. I can take the tape off his mouth and take him home with me," I protest.

"It looks like you have two dogs now. Your Great Dane and the little shih tzu don't want to be separated." He nods toward Big Boy and continues, "The tape crosses his whiskers and you don't want to pull those out. Besides, we'll have all the animals checked out—including the fighters in the other building."

"Big Boy looks fine," I attempt to argue.

Wayne says, "SOP—standard operating procedure. I'll see that you get Big Boy back as soon as possible."

He looks at me with a puzzled expression and then calls one of the deputies over.

"I know this is irregular, but I'm going to leave you officers to handle this for a short time while I take Ms. Parrish home myself."

The deputy's shocked expression doesn't change as Wayne escorts me to his patrol car.

A short while later, we are on the road to my apartment.

"You do realize that the reason I'm taking you home personally is because I love you and you seemed to think I was going to let that jerk shoot you."

"Did you figure Big Boy had been taken by dog fighters when he first disappeared?"

"I was afraid so. Like I told you, dog fighters use other dogs to train the pit bulls. A lot of the time, the bait dogs get killed in the battle. Other times, they're left to die, so I was worried, especially after I saw the tag on your fence."

"What kind of tag?" I ask.

"I told you about that. A touch of fluorescent paint on your gate. Dog fighters send scouts out looking for bait dogs during the day. When they spot a good candidate, they mark the place. Late at night, they come back and steal the dogs from marked residences."

"They took Big Boy during the day." I hope I don't sound too argumentative, but I can't resist saying this.

"He's so large that he would be prized to put in the ring with the pit bulls for training. May have marked your place several days ahead and grabbed him during the day when they realized that you take him in at night."

"Did coming for me mess up your plans to raid tonight's fight?"

"We'd planned to go in tonight during the

actual fight, but when I realized they had you, all that changed." His expression is solemn. "This is big, Callie. The fighters were in the other building. Usually, the fighting dogs and bait dogs are just tied to trees with heavy chains. They keep the operation out in the woods to hide the dogs because they make so much noise. This is a rather sophisticated operation with crates used for all the dogs. When they grabbed you, it went way beyond the fights though."

A deputy calls Wayne on his radio. I listen as the officer reports.

"Sheriff, we've found forty-seven pit bulls in all kinds of conditions. One of them has a broken leg that healed wrong and is permanently twisted. It's all swollen. A lot of them are bleeding from the face, the chest, and the leg areas. We'll carry them to the county animal shelter."

"Fine," Wayne responds and then asks, "What about the bait dogs?"

"The ones that were in the building with Miss Parrish hadn't been used yet. We're sending them to the rescue vet. They have owners who've been calling about missing animals. Once the vet okays each dog, it will be released to its owner or adopted out if no one claims it."

"I'll be right back," Wayne says.

"Everything's under control," the deputy tells him. "We found a separate room with scales, treadmills, weight gainers, and a stairway to train the dogs."

I listen as Wayne and the deputy sign off before asking, "Will the pit bulls be put up for adoption?"

"No, animals that have been conditioned and trained to fight can't be rehabilitated. They'll be euthanized."

I sit in silence while he drives. It seems petty and selfish, but my thoughts are on myself. I'm glad that Driver and Obee put me in the building with the bait dogs instead of the fight dogs. I don't want to see animals in the condition the deputy described.

"Do you have my phone?" I ask.

"Not with me, but you'll get it back. We found it slid under the passenger seat in your car."

"I didn't put it there. It must have wound up there when they ran into the back of my car," I say and then ask, "Should we call Allie and tell her I'm okay?"

"That's a good idea." He hands me his personal cell phone and adds, "I put her number on speed dial."

For just a moment, remembering how Allie looked in that red dress just last night, I feel a twinge of green in my eyes. Then I remember he said they'd been playing phone tag looking for me earlier.

Allie's line rings and rings and rings.

"She's not answering," I say.

"I'll take you out to her place tomorrow morning if I can get away," Wayne assures me. "I need to go back to the crime scene as soon as possible."

At my place, Wayne walks me inside, but it's obvious he's in a hurry to leave. I need someone to hold me, to tell me it's all going to be okay. Normally I'd call Jane, but Frankie's truck in the drive when Wayne and I drove up made that a less than great idea. Feeling like a little girl who wants her father, I wish I could call Daddy, but he and Miss Ellen spend all their time traveling since he married Miss Roadanza, so he's out of town. I don't even have Big Boy to hug for comfort.

I hit the shower and stay there until the hot water runs out. I crawl beneath the sheets and cry myself to sleep.

Sunday, November 1

Chapter 19

THE SLAMMING OF A DOOR wakes me the next morning. I hear my brother Frankie yell, "And this time I won't be back." Next is the roar of his truck engine followed by the squealing of tires.

After a quick trip to the bathroom, I call Jane on my landline, expecting her to be crying. Instead, she sounds chipper, downright joyful.

"Well, Callie, you can stop worrying about me and Frankie. He started in on me about working at Rizzie's. Says he doesn't want me in there everyday. He's so jealous he thinks I'm going to meet someone like Rizzie met Bob Everett. I can't win with him. He's jealous if I'm home talking on the phone, and he's jealous if I'm sweating in the kitchen at Rizzie's."

"Is that what you were arguing about this morning?"

"No, that was last night's argument. Finally he gave me an ultimatum to quit working for Rizzie, and then he went to sleep. I lay awake all night thinking about it. I do love him, Callie, or at least, I love him in a way, but not enough to put up with his crapola the rest of my life."

"Want me to come over for coffee and girl talk?"

"Sure. I'll make a fresh pot of Butterscotch-Toffee-flavored."

"Decaf?"

"Nope. I'll make the real thing for you." She giggles because this is a frequent discussion between us. She drinks so much coffee that she uses unleaded for herself. I like high test and need the caffeine.

I pull on a pair of jeans and a sweatshirt. When I reach Jane's front door, she opens it before I knock.

"Come on in. I miss you. It seems something is always in the way of our visiting like we used to."

"The 'something' is usually Wayne or Frankie."

"From now on, it will be only Wayne."

She goes to her single-cup coffeemaker and offers me the first cup before reloading it for herself. We sit at the breakfast table and Jane says, "I rolled around all night thinking about how it's been since Frankie and I first got together. I know he's your brother, but I don't think he'll ever grow up." She retrieves her own coffee and takes a sip.

"Now he's all upset because Rizzie says she's in love with Bob Everett. He says if someone can walk into the diner and sweep Rizzie off her feet, it could happen to me."

"That does seem unreasonable," I interject. "If you really love him, I don't think that will happen." I giggle. "Besides, you're hidden in the kitchen."

Jane bristles like she did in the old days. "Don't try to lay this on me, Calamine Lotion Parrish! Your brother has put me through pure h-e-double l. I spent the night thinking about how Bob Everett treats Rizzie and how Wayne treats you. Whatever Frankie feels for me, it's not love like they show you and Rizzie. Look at your dad, Callie. He really loves Miss Ellen or he wouldn't be traipsing off on all those trips to make her happy. We both know if he didn't love her, he'd be perfectly happy to stay home, cook, and play music. When I tried to explain that to Frankie, he went off on one of his temper tantrums."

"All I can say is I'm sorry, Jane." I apologize. "Sometimes I wonder if Wayne and I should be together. It seems to have happened too fast."

"Fast? You've known him your whole life."

"You know what I mean—becoming lovers instead of just long-time friends."

"Let's change the subject. Have you found Big Boy?"

We spend the next half hour with me telling Jane all that happened last night. Shock shows on her face.

"I'm worrying about my relationship with Frankie while you've been through all that?" She gives me a little hug. "To think I was even ticked at you last night because you didn't stay home to deal with trick-or-treaters."

"Are you working today?" I ask.

"Yes. Why don't you have another cup of coffee while I shower?"

I watch my best friend walk through her apartment as though she can see every piece of furniture. From the beginning of our friendship, I've been amazed how easily she moves through familiar turf without using her mobility cane. I forget how difficult some situations are for her.

Now, she's hurt about breaking up with my brother—again—but more than that, she's upset about what happened to me.

While Jane gets ready for work, I use her phone to try to call Allie again. Still no answer.

Jane comes out fully dressed with a towel wrapped around her head. She tugs it loose, bends over, and shakes her red curls before giving them a brisk rubbing. A quick comb-through and she's ready. She settles back in her chair with another cup of coffee, and I see tears slipping down her cheeks.

"Jane," I say, "are you okay?"

"No, I'm not. I'm not okay at all. I'm all bent

out of shape about Frankie while you could have been killed." The tears change from drops to a gushing waterfall.

I do the only thing I can do—what my work at the mortuary has taught me to do when someone is distraught. I put my arm around her shoulder and pat her.

A knock at the door causes me to slip my arm back and call out, "Who is it?"

"Is that you, Callie?" The voice is young and male—Tyrone.

"Yes, Ty." I open the door. He comes in while Jane wipes her face with a tissue from the box of Kleenex she keeps on the table in the same place all the time.

"I've come to pick up Jane for work. I figured you were gone off. Where's your car?"

"Impounded again."

With the loudness that comes with his youth and gender, Tyrone laughs. "Again? Who did you find dead this time?"

"The sheriff found me. The people who stole Big Boy kidnapped me."

"The ones who were dog-fighting?"

"Yes, how do you know about that?"

"It's all over the news."

"Please tell me they didn't give my name."

"Nope, not this time." He grins. "Do you want to ride with us to the grill?"

"Sure. I'm hungry. Do you think after I eat breakfast Rizzie would let you take me over to see

---

Allie? Wayne said he'll take me, but I have an idea he's going to be all tied up with his sheriff responsibilities today, and I can't get Allie on the telephone."

"I'd say yes if you ask Rizzie." He bounces to another subject. "Do you know anything about the principal's death? There are all kinds of rumors, but if they're true, I don't understand closing the school for a week in his honor."

"I don't know any of the details."

"I thought maybe the sheriff had told you something."

"You know Wayne would never give out confidential police information."

WHEN WE ENTER GASTRIC GULLAH GRILL, I'm not surprised to see Bob Everett sitting in his favorite booth reading the newspaper. The headline is so bold that it seems to jump off the page:

$100,000 DOG FIGHTING RING BUSTED ON COAST OF SOUTH CAROLINA

"Did you see this?" Bob asks me as Jane heads for the kitchen. "It says some stolen dogs have been recovered. Do you think your pet is one of them?"

"He is. Big Boy is at the vet's, but I hope to get him back later today."

"Have a seat. Rizzie will be out as soon as she goes over the entrée specials with Jane."

I slide in across the table from Bob. Tyrone goes behind the counter and calls, "Coffee, Callie?"

"No, thanks, but I'd love a glass of water," I answer Ty and then turn toward Bob. "What's going on with you?" I ask, not wanting to get into a description of everything that happened to me the day before.

"Actually, quite a lot. Analysis of the skull Tyrone found over by the school is far from complete, but the age and characteristics determined so far support the theory that it's from an extinct Native American group thought to have inhabited this region. Unless that proves false, I'll be staying here quite a while working with the excavation of that field. It could be a very important archaeological find."

I look up and see Rizzie come from the kitchen and head toward us.

"Don't be flirting with my man, Callie," Rizzie jokes.

"I have my own, thank you," I reply. "We were talking about the skull Ty found."

"Yes, Bob told me about that." She slides in beside him and plants a little kiss on his cheek. "But still nothing positive about the skull and flowers found at the old Halsey place, right?"

I tell her and Bob what Zack told me about his putting the skull and flowers there planning to "find" it and use it to promote the TEAM's haunted house. I don't mention lightning striking the Halsey house. I'm not aware who, if anyone, knows yet that the building burned. The Halsey property is kind of far out and has, or should I say had, no close neighbors. I did change my mind about not reporting the fire after I realized how terrible it would be if the woods caught fire, so I notified the fire department after telling Zack not to report it.

"Changing the subject, Rizzie, is it okay for Tyrone to drive me to see Allie Patterson this morning? I was headed there yesterday, but I got sidetracked and now she's not answering her phone."

I don't mention that I've developed some concerns that I'd like to discuss with Allie. I don't have any idea what she wants to talk with me about, could be about how to correct her hair color and get the green out of the strawberry blond. When I questioned her about the green and whether she'd been in a pool with chlorine at the bed-and-breakfast, she acted offended. Could the slight green discoloration in her hair be from the fire chief's hot tub?

Can Allie have had anything to do with the deaths of the three men who have died in St. Mary since she returned? I know. I've dealt with so many homicides that I suspect murder too often. Maybe it's coincidence. But then, Wayne says there's never coincidence, just crime.

"Sure. Let me check with Jane and see if she needs Ty to pick up anything while he's out."

Rizzie stands and heads for the kitchen.

"Excuse me for a few minutes," Bob says and goes to the men's room.

When Rizzie returns, she sits across from me.

"Really not my business, but are you and Bob seeing each other out of the diner?" I ask.

"You already know that," Rizzie answers and her face fills with happiness. "He's exactly the man I've always wanted, and don't you dare say anything about father fixations."

"I'm not. I'm happy for you. I just can't help remembering something your grandmother told us not long after I met her."

"What's that?"

"Play with fire, you may get burned. Rob the cradle, you may get pooped on."

Rizzie laughed. "I remember her telling you that, but this is different. He's not robbing the cradle. I'm robbing the rocking chair."

I join her in laughing at this. When Bob and Ty both reappear at the booth, we don't bother to explain our mirth.

"WHERE TO?" TY ASKS as he pulls the van out of the parking lot.

"I'll direct you. Allie rented Cabin Eight at Hidden Lake. I think I know how to get there, but if not, you have GPS on your phone, don't you?"

"I've got GPS, but I know how to get to Hidden Lake." He laughs, and I remember hearing that local teenagers liked to park there.

"May I use your cell to try Allie again?"

"Where's your phone?"

"Long story, but I should get it back soon. If not, I'll have to buy another one. I might even upgrade."

Ty takes his cell from his pocket and hands it to me.

Again, I try Allie, but there's still no answer.

Tyrone pulls over, stops the van, and turns on his MP3 player through the van's radio.

"Do you mind if we listen to this?" he asks.

"Not at all," I assure him. I love most music, and no matter what plays, it will be better than silence. The quiet is opening my mind to too much—thinking about yesterday and last night and then turning to why Allie isn't answering her phone.

"What's wrong?" Tyrone asks. "If you don't like the music, I'll change it."

"No, I'm just worried about Allie. I was supposed to visit her at the cabin yesterday afternoon, but I wasn't able to go. She called Wayne, but since then, she hasn't answered my calls or his."

"Maybe she forgot to charge her phone." He looks around. "Or maybe when she got to this wooded paradise, she decided to chill with Mother Nature and turned off her phone."

That might be true except that if Allie called the sheriff because I didn't arrive, she'd been concerned. If she's worried at all, I don't think she's turned off the phone.

Hidden Lake Road twists and turns through a dense, wooded section with Spanish moss hanging so thick and heavy that it feels like we're riding through a tunnel. It ends at the lake, but a developer has built cabins all along the road. I say "along" the road, but actually they're visible while driving but set back to give some privacy. Parking spaces are provided near the pavement, making it necessary to walk down wooded paths to the cabins.

"She said she's in Cabin Eight," I say when we pass Cabin Six. The buildings all look the same—wooden structures painted to look like log cabins.

Ty drives past the seventh building and then turns into the parking area labeled Cabin Eight. He parks beside the rental car I recognize as the one Allie had the last time I saw her. We get out of the van and walk up the path to the front porch. No more than twenty feet from the steps, Ty gasps. I look down and see what has taken his breath.

Fletcher Williams lies on the ground. He's on his back with his hands clutched over his abdomen. Reddish-brown blood stains creep from beneath his fingers. Fletch's face is distorted—mouth open in the exact same gaping expression as I've seen at the wax museum in Myrtle Beach. He looks just like Lee Harvey Oswald did at the moment he was shot. A handgun lies beside

Fletch.

"Call 911," I tell Ty while I check Fletcher's pulse, though I've seen enough bodies to know he's dead. The smell of liquor is strong.

"I'm not ever going anywhere with you again, Callie," Tyrone says when he finishes talking to dispatch. "You keep finding bodies." He looks down at Fletcher. "I've got some tablecloths in the van. I was taking them home to wash. Should I get one and cover him up?"

"No, that might disturb evidence. Let's see if Allie is inside."

My mind races. I'd suspected Allie of being in the hot tub with Norman Clark because of the green discoloration of her hair, not an uncommon phenomenon when blond hair is in water with too much chlorination. That has led me to question if Melvin Barnes hanged himself in his office after the reunion or if Allie had been part of that, too. Did she shoot Fletcher Williams? If so, she hasn't escaped in the rental car.

Ty beats on the cabin door, but no one comes, and there is no sound from inside. After a few minutes, he leans hard against the door and it opens. We both step inside. The interior is simple, furnished with plain furniture, but clean and neat.

"Allie," I call.

"Ms. Patterson," Ty shouts.

No answer. We go into the kitchen. Nobody there. Ty pushes open a closed door and steps through. He yells my name.

"Callie, come here," he shouts.

Tyrone's eyes bug out and his mouth drops open.

Allie lies on the bed on top of the covers with her head on a pillow. Her arms extend beside her, and the left one has a syringe hanging from the inner elbow. I pick up her wrist and feel for a pulse. There is none. Ty lifts a blue notebook from beside her right hand, opens it, and holds it in front of my face while leaning over my shoulder.

VENDETTA
by Alice Lara Patterson

"Vendetta? What does that mean?" Tyrone asks me.

"Revenge," I say as I begin CPR. "A series of acts performed by someone to get revenge."

There's obviously no reaction to the CPR. In reality, rigor mortis has begun to set in, and I know that Allie is gone for good. Ty turns the page and together we read Allie's manuscript:

On Senior Cut Day twenty-seven years ago, I was at the beach with most of the other seniors until late that afternoon. My sister Josie, almost seven, went bike-riding on the country roads close around our farm just like she usually did after school. When she didn't come home in time for supper, our family went looking for her. Mom found Josie's dead body on the side of the road— a victim of hit-and-run. The coroner said Josie bled out slowly. If the driver had stopped and called an ambulance, there was a chance Josie could have been saved. I am the sole survivor of our family. I stayed away for years and returned to see if I could bear to live in the family farm house and write a book.

My 27th high school class reunion was the first night I was here. I dressed in red, wanting to be noticed by everyone. Fletch Williams was drunk and puked on the floor. His high school buddies, Melvin Barnes, Norman Clark, and Sammy Bee rushed him out of the gym when he began mumbling about guilt.

On the pretense of going to the ladies' room, I followed them and eavesdropped outside Principal Barnes's office. Fletch was telling them that he never told that the four of them were in the car that hit Josie, and he was obviously filled with guilt. None of them denied killing my sister. They only wanted to quiet Fletcher. Three of them had become respected members of the community, and the only one who seemed to even care that they went joy-riding on Senior Cut Day and killed Josie was Fletcher Williams.

My vendetta began that very night. I flirted with Melvin Barnes and promised him privileges after the reunion. When everyone was gone, we went to his office, and I convinced him to try some kinky acts. One of them involved limiting his oxygen during sex. He allowed me to tie a jump rope around his neck. I yanked it and watched as his face turned blue. I kept pulling and he died. Score one for the vendetta.

The second to die was Fire Chief Norman Clark. I went by the fire department and pretended I wanted to talk to him about Melvin's death. One thing led to another, and we wound up in his hot tub together that evening. I complained about mosquitoes and suggested he move the bug light from over the patio to a branch over the hot tub. When he was standing on the edge of the tub, reaching up to hook the zapper over the light, I hit him in the back as hard as I could with a piece of two by four that had been beside the garage. Norman and the bug light fell into the hot tub together. I turned and ran out without waiting to see and hear what happened next. Now I hear that his body has been sent for an autopsy. This must mean someone is questioning how he died. I've heard that Callie solves a lot of murders. Does she suspect me?

At Norman's visitation, I talked to Sammy Bee about buying a car. He wanted to talk about me and Melvin at the reunion, but I assured him there was nothing to that and also convinced him I knew nothing about Norman's death either. I agreed to meet him early the next morning with Callie, but after the dealership closed, I called and arranged to see him that night. While promises of sexual *favors had worked with Melvin and Norman, Sammy wasn't interested. All he wanted was to sell me an expensive car.*

When I went to Hidden Lake and rented my cabin, I found some leftover flexible dryer vent material and duct tape in the kitchen where they connected appliances. Those careless workmen had left a small tool chest in the garage. That stuff gave me an idea, and I put all of it in the trunk of my rented car. I'd planned to be seductive with Sammy like I was with Melvin and Norman, but he wasn't at all interested. He kept telling me he was happily married. I asked him for a drink, but all he had was coffee and sodas. I slipped a couple of sleeping pills into his coffee. After he went sound asleep sitting at the desk in his office, I backed his Camaro up to the outer door and attached one end of the dryer vent to the car exhaust and the other end to a small hole I made in the sliding door with a glass cutter from the tool chest.

Fletcher was the easiest of all. He'd spent all those years feeling guilty. All I did with him was bring him to my cabin and get him drunk. I gave him a loaded pistol and locked him out. I don't know if he fired the shot on purpose or stumbled, but when I went out to look, he was dead. Less than a week since I came here, the four men who killed my baby sister and destroyed my family are dead.

Callie, thank you for being my friend. I hope you won't have hard feelings about me. Do you realize that you are the age Josie would be if she'd lived? I simply needed someone to talk to, and being with you was kind of like being with Josie all grown up.

I thought I could get revenge for Josie's death and no one ever know that the four musketeers didn't cause their own deaths, but I know you've begun to suspect me. You questioned the green tinge of chlorine I couldn't get out of my hair, and now Norman is having an autopsy. You may be the cause of that, too. Before long, you would have put all the deaths together and tied the blame to me.

Please don't think of me as a murderer. I wanted you to come up last night to confess to you. Yes, my sister's four killers died by my hand, but these were not murders. They were executions— executions that had been delayed 27 years. Melvin was hanged by the neck until dead. Norman was electrocuted. Sam slept himself to oblivion in my version of the gas chamber, and poor Fletcher died by firing squad. I didn't kill them; I executed them.

Now, it is my turn. When you find this story of my vendetta, you will discover me also—dead by lethal injection for taking the law into my own hands. Think of my death as capital punishment for the capital punishment I inflicted on the men who took my sister's life. My vendetta is ended.

Attached to Allie's Vendetta is her will— leaving me the farm she inherited from her father. As her heir, I will have her buried beside Josie and mark her final resting place with a larger but similar angel to Josie's.

Will I ever try to refurbish the house and live there? I don't know. So far, I haven't even found the nerve to go out and inspect the property. Tyrone tells me he went and looked. He thinks it will make a super place for the TEAM class to use for their haunted house next year.

Jane's Ground Meat Cookbook

In previous Callie Parrish books, Frankie took it upon himself to publish recipes from Pa Parrish and Rizzie Profit. Frankie is no longer in good grace, and Callie refuses to let him do that again. Instead, here are some of the recipes Jane chose for her cookbook.

MAELENE'S SCHOOL VEGETABLE SOUP

Maelene Johnson is a retired school cafeteria worker who lives in Raleigh, North Carolina. This is the recipe used for vegetable soup when she worked for the school system.

INGREDIENTS

1 tablespoon butter or oil
2 or 3 pounds lean ground beef
1 or 2 medium onions, chopped
2 stalks celery, sliced
1 28-ounce can diced tomatoes
1 14.5 ounce can tomato sauce*
1 pound package frozen mixed vegetables**
1 or 2 medium potatoes, peeled and chopped chunky
3 teaspoons pepper
2 teaspoons salt

1 teaspoon dried oregano
2 ½ quarts water

DIRECTIONS

Brown meat in large pot with the butter. Remove meat. Add onions and celery and saute briefly. Stir in all other ingredients and allow to simmer at least an hour, preferably longer.

*Though the school system used tomato sauce in soup, at home Maelene substitutes sixteen ounces of V-8 juice. "Makes it even better," she advises.

**Leftover or fresh vegetables can be used instead of frozen. Addition of butter beans is excellent.

Maelene says that she serves this with corn bread, but the traditional menu at schools had peanut butter sandwiches with soup. The peanut butter was slightly sweetened and smoothed by adding a bit of honey or syrup to it before making sandwiches.

KAREN COOK'S HAMBURGER/SQUASH CASSEROLE

Karen is the retired owner of The Gator Restaurant, which was in operation from 1988 until 2007 in Lake View, South Carolina. Her cookbook, *Karen's Casual Cooking* features favorites served at the restaurant. Karen says, "I like simple cooking. The fresher the vegetables, the better the taste." This dish was a surefire sellout every time the restaurant offered it.

Ingredients

10-12 medium summer squash
1 medium onion, chopped
2 cups grated cheddar cheese
2 pounds hamburger meat
1 can cream of mushroom soup
Salt and pepper to taste
1 cup milk

Directions

Wash and cut up squash. Boil with onion until tender. Drain. Put squash/onion mixture in bottom of greased casserole dish. Heat cheese, soup, and milk until cheese melts. Brown meat. Drain well. Place hamburger on top of squash mixture. Pour cheese and mushroom mix over top.
Heat in oven at 325 degrees for about 15 minutes. Enjoy!

EDNA ANDERSON'S CHEESEBURGER GRITS

Edna is a retired educator and world traveler. She's accomplished in many advanced fields including cooking, but this simple invention is a favorite of Rev. Russell Anderson, Edna's husband, a retired Lutheran pastor. He is also fond of baked macaroni and cheese.

Ingredients

Cooked grits*
Pre-fried hamburger meat
Grated cheese

Directions

Quantities are not specific. Prepare enough grits to serve however many will be eating. Add approximately one crumbled cooked hamburger patty and several tablespoons of cheese per person. Stir ingredients together. Serve. This is so simple, but oh, so good.

*Edna uses stone-ground grits. When they are cooked, she adds crumbled cooked hamburger meat and grated cheese to taste. Chef's preference as to kind of cheese. Edna's husband, Pastor Russell Anderson, prefers cheddar.

This is one of the few dishes that Callie prepares. Of course, she adapts it *a'la Callie Parrish.*

CALLIE'S VERSION

Ingredients

Instant grits prepared by directions on packet*
One leftover hamburger patty—crumbled
One mounded tablespoon Cheez Whiz

Instant grits are better if made with milk instead of water. Callie uses plain, butter, or cheese grits.

Directions

Stir it all up. Eat it all up.

NOTE FROM JANE BAKER

After two very simple recipes, we move to a more complicated one that is worth every bit of the effort.

JENNY'S PASTITSIO

Jenny Stallings from Lexington, SC, finds time for creative cooking as well as home-schooling her children (she has seven) and spending time with her first grandchild. Any dish from Jenny's kitchen is sure to please everyone at her table. Her pastitsio is a three-step recipe, but it's a definite winner!

Ingredients

2 large onions, chopped fine
¼ cup butter
2 pounds lean ground beef
2 teaspoons salt
¼ teaspoon pepper
1 8-ounce can tomato sauce
1 cup water
½ teaspoon ground cinnamon
Pinch of sugar

½ cup bread crumbs
2 ½ cups grated Parmesan cheese
1 pound elbow macaroni
2 tablespoons olive oil
3 tablespoons melted butter
Cream sauce (see recipe below)

Directions

STEP ONE – MEAT SAUCE

Prepare sauce by browning ground beef and onion in butter. Drain. Add salt, pepper, tomato sauce, water, cinnamon, and sugar. Simmer forty-five minutes. Remove from heat. When cool, add half the bread crumbs and 1 ¼ cups cheese to meat mixture.

STEP TWO – CREAM SAUCE

Ingredients

1 cup butter
½ cup all-purpose flour
6 cups warm milk
Pinch of nutmeg
6 whole eggs
½ cup grated Parmesan cheese

Directions

Melt butter and blend in flour, stirring constantly. Add warm milk gradually while stirring until sauce thickens. Stir in nutmeg. Remove from heat and cool. Beat eggs with wire whisk. Add ½ cup of cooled sauce to eggs and stir well. Pour egg mixture into cream sauce and stir in cheese.

Assembly

Cook macaroni in boiling, salted water with olive oil until almost done. Rinse and drain well.

Preheat oven to 350 degrees. Butter bottom of 11 x 17-inch baking dish and sprinkle with two tablespoons of bread crumbs. Spread half of macaroni on bottom and sprinkle ½ cup cheese over it. Cover with meat mixture. Pour half of cream sauce over the meat. Spread remaining macaroni over cream sauce and top with the rest of the meat sauce. Sprinkle with remaining bread crumbs and cheese. Bake at 350 degrees for fifty minutes or until golden brown.

DOTTIE'S PORCUPINE MEATBALLS

Submitted by Dottie Jones, music teacher from Lexington, SC. Dottie says these are a throwback to the seventies, but are still crowd-pleasers, especially with children who love the looks of the rice sticking out which is the origin of the name.

Ingredients

1 lb. ground beef
½ cup uncooked long-grain white rice
1 tsp. salt

¼ tsp. pepper
Dash of chili powder
1 medium onion, sliced thin
½ green pepper, sliced thin
1 Tbsp. fat*
2 ½ tomato sauce (#300 can)

Directions

Mix beef, rice, salt, pepper, and chili powder. Set aside. Put onion, green peppers and fat* into skillet and cook 15 minutes. Add tomato sauce to the veggies. Form meat mixture into balls and drop into tomato sauce in skillet. Turn occasionally while cooking meatballs in sauce. Cook until meat is done (approximately 20 minutes.).

*Dottie asked should we change the word "fat," which probably would not appear in this recipe if written now. The editor vetoed that idea. When the recipe was created, "fat" probably referred to lard, but these days, most cooks would use vegetable oil or olive oil to make it healthier.

SIMPLE MEXICAN MEAT LOAF OR MEATBALLS

Submitted by Evelyn Baker of Rembert, SC, who claims her recipes are "easy enough for Callie."

Ingredients

2 pounds ground beef
2 slices bread

2 eggs
½ cup milk
1 envelope taco seasoning

Directions

Beat eggs with milk. Pour over bread and leave until bread is soggy. Stir in seasoning mix and then add meat. Combine thoroughly before patting into a 4" x 8" loaf pan. Bake at 350 degrees for one hour. To make meatballs instead of meat loaf, roll raw meat mixture into small balls and either pan fry or bake for thirty minutes. Serve with salsa and cheese.

ANGEE'S FAST AND EASY SUPPER

Twelve-year-old Angee Carter is a student in Greenville, SC. Two of her favorite activities are reading and cooking. She submitted this recipe with a note: "My brothers and sister love this recipe when I double it and feed the whole family."

Ingredients

1 pound ground beef
1 medium onion, chopped
1 tablespoon olive oil
1 can cream of celery soup
¼ cup soy sauce
1 small can chopped or sliced water chestnuts
Cooked rice or canned Chinese noodles

Directions

Brown meat and onion in olive oil. Drain off grease. Mix in cream of celery soup, water, and soy sauce. Simmer a few minutes until warm and well blended. Stir in water chestnuts and serve over rice or noodles.

About The Author

FRAN RIZER'S magazine features have been published in *Better Homes & Gardens, South Carolina Magazine, Field & Stream, Living Blues, Bluegrass Unlimited, Bluegrass Now,* and others. After retirement from teaching, she ventured into fiction and was a winner in the Augusta, Georgia, Porter Fleming Fiction Contest. Rizer's short fiction has been published in the USA and Canada, and her Callie Parrish mysteries have been nominated for SIBA and Agatha Awards.

A Skull Full of Posies is Rizer's eighth in the Callie Parrish mystery series. Her first thriller, *KUDZU RIVER—A Thriller of Abuse, Murder, & Retribution* was released in 2015. *Southern Swamps & Ruins,* a collaborative anthology of ghost stories, with Richard D. Laudenslager, was published in 2016. *The Horror of Julie Bates,* Rizer's venture into the horror genre, was also released in 2016.

Rizer is a featured author on the SCETV series, *A Literary Tour of South Carolina,* on *Streamline* which is offered to all South Carolina public schools. Check out www.franrizer.com or see the Internet for links to interviews and reviews. She lives in South Carolina near her two sons, Nathan and Adam, and her grandson Aeden Rizer.

50470036R00157

Made in the USA
Middletown, DE
31 October 2017